TEN TALES OF CHRISTMAS

Selected by
LYNNE G. MILLER

Illustrated by
ROBERT J. LEE

SCHOLASTIC INC.
New York Toronto London Auckland Sydney

For permission to reprint the poems and stories included in TEN TALES OF CHRISTMAS, appreciation is expressed to the following publishers and authors:

CHILD LIFE Magazine for "Colin's Christmas Candle" by Barbara Raferty, copyright 1956.

Collins Publishers for Canadian and British Commonwealth rights to "Paddington's Christmas" from MORE ABOUT PADDINGTON by Michael Bond, illustrations by Peggy Fortnum.

Doubleday and Company, Inc. for "The Story of the Christmas Spider" by Marguerite de Angeli from UP THE HILL, copyright © 1942 by Marguerite de Angeli.

E. P. Dutton & Co. and the author for "One Night" by Marchette Chute from RHYMES ABOUT THE COUNTRY, copyright 1946 by Marchette Chute.

Aileen Fisher for "December" from THAT'S WHY, Thomas Nelson & Sons, N.Y. 1946.

Hallmark Cards for "I Could Eat It" by Issa from EASTERN CULTURE, Vol. I, by R. H. Blyth. © Hallmark Cards, Inc.

Harper & Row, Publishers, Inc. for "The Christmas Horses" by Laura Ingalls Wilder, abridged from Chapter 12 and Chapter 13 in ON THE BANKS OF PLUM CREEK, copyright 1937 by Harper & Brothers; renewed copyright © 1964 by Roger L. MacBride.

The Hokuseido Press, Tokyo, Japan for "I Could Eat it" by Issa from HAIKU, Vols. I-IV, edited and translated by R. H. Blyth.

Houghton Mifflin Company for "Paddington's Christmas," Chapter 7 from MORE ABOUT PADDINGTON by Michael Bond, illustrations by Peggy Fortnum. Text copyright © 1959 by Michael Bond, illustrations copyright © 1959 by Peggy Fortnum.

International Famous Agency for "Perfect Present" by Dr. Seuss, copyright © 1953 by Theodore Geisel.

The Macmillan Company for "City Christmas" by Rachel Field from POEMS, copyright 1934 by The Macmillan Company, renewed 1962 by Arthur S. Pederson.

Methuen & Co. Ltd. for British Commonwealth rights to "The Christmas Horses" by Laura Ingalls Wilder from ON THE BANKS OF PLUM CREEK.

Platt & Munk Publishers for "Baboushka" from FAVORITE STORIES FOR THE CHILDREN'S HOUR by Bailey & Lewis, copyright by Platt & Munk Publishers © 1965.

Russell & Volkening, Inc. for "A Christmas Tree for Lydia" by Elizabeth Enright, copyright © 1947, 1951 by Elizabeth Enright Gillham.

Scholastic Magazines, Inc. for "The Christmas Gift" by Vic Crume, copyright © 1972 by Vic Crume; "Angel in the Snow" by Vic Crume, copyright © 1972 by Vic Crume; music by Linda S. Williams, copyright © 1972 by Linda S. Williams; and "Sing a Song of Tinsel" by Dorothy N. Morrison, © 1965 by Scholastic Magazines, Inc.

Margaret Tuttle for "The Christmas Foundling," copyright © 1963 by CHILD LIFE Magazine.

Frederick Ungar Publishing Co., Inc. for "Cosette's Christmas" by Victor Hugo, abridgement by Claire Huchet Bishop in HAPPY CHRISTMAS!, copyright 1956 by Stephen Daye Press.

ISBN 0-590-41447-X

12 11 10 9 8 7 6 5 4 3 11 8 9/8 0 1 2/9

CONTENTS

To Nancy and Hilda and Irving,
all of whom live the Christmas
Spirit throughout the year.

Colin's Christmas Candle

Colin walked slowly home from school, scuffing his feet as he crossed the hill of the little Irish fishing village. It did not seem like Christmas Eve. Perhaps this was because it had not yet snowed.

But Colin knew there was another reason why it did not seem like Christmas — a reason he did not dare even whisper in his heart.

He looked out across the lead-colored sea. There was not a speck of a ship on the horizon. And seven days ago his father's fishing schooner had been due home.

"I'll bring you a sheepdog pup from the Shetland Isles," Colin's father had said when he left. "You'll have it a week before Christmas, I am certain." But tonight was Christmas Eve.

Colin looked toward the lighthouse, high on the hill. Seven days ago a north gale had short-circuited the lighthouse wires, and snuffed out the great light. For seven days there had been no beam to guide a schooner home.

Colin pushed open the cottage door. He heard his mother moving in the kitchen. "We'll need more peat for the fire, Colin," she said as she came into the front room. "And it's nearly time to light the candle for the Christ Child."

"I'm not caring much about lighting a candle, Mother," he said.

"I know, for I'm not caring much either," replied his mother. "But everybody in Ireland lights a candle on Christmas Eve. Even when there's sadness in the house. It is a symbol that your house and heart are open to poor strangers. Come now, I've two candles, one for each of us. If you gather some peat, we'll be ready for supper soon."

Colin went outside to gather the peat. "I'm not caring much about lighting a candle," he repeated to himself as he glanced toward the lighthouse, "when there's not so much as a beam of light to guide a schooner home."

But while Colin was staring at the lighthouse, an idea hit him like a gust of wind. He turned and started running up the long hill to the lighthouse. He pounded on the door and Mr. Duffy, the keeper, opened it a crack.

"What's got into you, young fellow, startling an old man like me — and on Christmas Eve too?"

"Mr. Duffy," gasped Colin, "how did you used to light the lighthouse? Could you do it again?"

"Why, the electric batteries are blown, my boy. Dead as can be! And none to be bought from here to Dublin."

"I mean, how did you light the lighthouse before there were such things as batteries?"

"Why, by the oil lamp that's buried in the cellar. Now what wild thing have ye in mind? There's no oil kept here now." Mr. Duffy stared at Colin and then lowered his voice. "Sure, 'tis your father you're thinking of, if he's one of those on the lost schooner. . . ."

"Would kerosene light the lamp?"

"Well, I suppose," Mr. Duffy mused. "But don't go getting any ideas in your head, lad. I'd like to see anyone find a spare quart of kerosene in this village, much less enough to. . ."

Colin was gone before Mr. Duffy could finish his sentence.

Down, down the hill he ran, back to the cottage. Quickly he gathered four pails from the kitchen and darted for the door. His mother ran after him to the steps. "Colin, 'tis time to light . . . Colin!" But he was gone.

Colin knew that a candle in an Irish home on Christmas Eve meant that any stranger coming to the door would be welcomed *and given whatever he asked!* It was five o'clock now, and he could see candles beginning to glow in every cottage in the valley below him. He didn't stop running until he came to the first house.

"Could you spare me but half a cup of kerosene from your lamp?" he asked. "Have you any kerosene in your cellar?" Colin went to every house where a candle shone in the window.

In one hour he had filled two pails. Slowly and painfully he carted them up to the lighthouse door.

He knocked. Mr. Duffy appeared, and stared.

"What manner of miracle is this?" he asked. "This is enough to keep the lamp burning for the night."

"I'll get more yet," Colin shouted, as he started down the hill. "It's early still."

After two more long hours, Colin had gathered two more pails of kerosene. When he was halfway up the hill for the second time, he saw the tower suddenly flicker

with light. A great beam spread out over the valley, and stretched toward the dark heart of the sea. Mr. Duffy had lighted the lamp!

When Colin reached home it was very late. His mother jumped from her seat near the fire.

"Colin, where have you been? You've had no supper, nor lighted your candle!"

"I've lighted a candle, Mother, and a big one! It's a secret, and I can't tell you yet. But it was a huge candle indeed!"

After that, Colin ate his supper and went quietly to bed.

He dreamed all night of candles, and fishing schooners, and kegs and kegs of oil. Then a great shouting aroused him from his sleep.

"The ship has come in! The ship has come in! 'Twas the light, they say — that Mr. Duffy lighted. They were but ten miles out all week after the storm, just drifting in the fog."

Colin opened his eyes. He saw that dawn was breaking and that his mother was standing at the door. He bounded from bed and pulled on his clothes, then ran to the door and looked toward the harbor. It was true then! There was the schooner with its rigging standing out against the gray of the sea.

Colin raced for the harbor. He felt a moist wind in his face. It was beginning to snow. Oh, it was Christmas all right, falling from heaven and right into his heart!

Barbara Raferty

9

ONE NIGHT

Last winter when the snow was deep
    And sparkled on the lawn
And there was moonlight everywhere,
    I saw a little fawn.

I watched her playing in the snow.
    She did not want to leave.
She must have known before she came
    That it was Christmas Eve.

Marchette Chute

Sing a Song of Tinsel

Elsa lay shivering in a cold bed, feet drawn up and wrapped in the skirt of her flannel nightgown. Cringing at the chill, rough touch of the cotton blanket, she stretched her toes toward the heated soapstone, inched it closer, wrapped her feet again and lay quiet. At last she grew warm and turned over to sob noiselessly into her pillow. Susan in the next room must not hear and wonder why she was crying on Christmas night.

Through the floor register from the room below Elsa could hear the whine of the victrola, a sporadic crackling as her father enjoyed his bowl of holiday nuts, and an occasional shout of high-pitched laughter from her mother and Aunt Laura. At least, thought Elsa, she had kept so cheerful — even gay — all the day long that no one had guessed her shame. No one, she thought, would ever know why a limp red thread would always hang from her violin.

Seven years earlier, on a hot August day, an enormous tent had stood in the village park of Chautauqua. When Grandfather had offered to let Elsa, age seven, use

11

his ticket for one of the concerts, she was thrilled. She told her best friend Sarah, but Sarah sneered.

"You're not supposed to use anybody else's ticket," she said. "*I* have my own."

"Grandpa said I could."

"That doesn't matter." Sarah shook her head. "Tickets aren't meant for anyone but the person that buys them. My mother said so."

"Just the same, I'm going." Elsa swallowed hard. Could it be so wrong?

The next day Elsa went to Chautauqua with Grandmother. As they approached the tent she held back and eyed the man who was punching tickets. He turned each one around and around, tilting his head to squint through the bottom part of his glasses. Would he notice Grandfather's name written out so plainly? She jerked at her grandmother's elbow.

"Maybe — maybe the man won't let me in on Grandfather's ticket."

Grandmother laughed. "Guess it's up to your grandpa how he uses it."

Elsa's heart pounded as Grandmother handed over the tickets, but the man only punched them with a sharp click and returned them, smiling.

Elsa breathed more easily. He hadn't noticed. Of course Grandmother had known all along that he wouldn't have time to read the name on each. And now they were safely past the door.

Inside the tent Elsa marveled at the crowd of people and their buzz of excitement.

When the crimson curtain at last parted, a small orchestra began to play, the first Elsa had ever heard. She leaned toward the aisle to watch the violinist, a young lady in white with a long dark curl that hung in front of her shoulder. She swayed with the music and tossed back her curl, but when she bowed at the end of each solo she raised a graceful hand to draw it forward again. Her pieces were gay — sad — sweet — brilliant. Elsa was entranced.

"I'm going to play a violin! Somehow I'll get one," she promised herself.

She thought about it as she trotted home beside Grandmother, only half hearing the comfortable old voice at her side. That evening after supper she told her parents about it.

"My father played a violin," Mother said. "He brought it all the way from Germany. But it was stolen." She sighed. "I don't know how we could get you another, Elsa, with the store just getting started. Maybe — later — " Her voice faltered.

"I could earn some money," suggested Elsa. "You have so much mending. I'll sew all the buttons."

Mother shook her head. "That would be too hard, Elsa."

Elsa turned to her father. "Maybe I could help in the store."

Father smiled at her over his newspaper. "What could you do there?"

"I can count money. I could sell things."

"And weigh nails? And measure rope? And lift stoves? 'Fraid not, dear. It takes a man to handle hardware." He slipped his arm around her waist.

"Could I have some money instead of a birthday present?"

"We might manage that — a little. I'd buy you a violin if I could, Elsa, but times are hard now."

After that Elsa did not coax, but sometimes when she was alone she pretended to be a violinist. They had some violin records which she played. Then with two yardsticks for violin and bow, she smiled and bowed for her invisible audience.

One day she was scraping away with the yardsticks when Mother came home early. "Elsa!" she exclaimed.

Elsa dropped the yardsticks and her face grew hot.

Her mother walked toward her. "Do you still want to play a violin?"

Without answer Elsa ran upstairs to her room, banged shut the door and flung herself on the bed.

14

Her mother followed. "We understand — Father and I," she said. "Only we can't manage it just now."

"You didn't have to watch me," Elsa sobbed.

"I'm sorry — I didn't know — " Mother's eyes were full of tears.

Never again did Elsa play with the yardsticks.

The family often took a ride in the square, high old-fashioned car which Father so carefully washed and greased every Sunday morning. Summer evenings they drove along the Little Cedar River to watch the fireflies. In the fall they drove through the wooded hills that blazed with red and gold. But rides through the winter snow were best of all. Snugly wrapped in auto robes they watched the falling flakes brush against the windshield. Often, if the store had had a good week, Father would stop at the popcorn wagon.

It was there that Elsa saved money. "I'd rather have a nickel," she would say.

"Don't you want any popcorn?" Father was amazed.

"No — I'd rather have the money."

"You can't be begging from others." He reached into his pocket for some coins.

"I won't. Not even a kernel. Please. I promise." The eager words came in a rush. "I'd *really* rather have the nickel."

"Um-m," Father hesitated. "What do you think, Mother?"

Mother sounded tired. "You know — she thinks she can save up for a violin."

"All right, let her try. It won't last, anyway."

So Elsa received a nickel and held it in her palm all the rest of the ride, hearing in her heart the song of a violin. The popcorn smelled good, it sounded good, but not a kernel did she beg. Nor was any offered to her.

Father was wrong. The plan lasted — and lasted — with Elsa always waiting patiently for the blissful moment when everyone's popcorn was gone, but the nickel — warm, round, hard — was still in her hand.

Slowly her little hoard grew until she had more than nine dollars. She kept it in a small tin box, counting it out sometimes and arranging it in neat stacks of pennies, nickels, dimes, a few quarters, and even a dollar bill.

One day Mother returned from a hurried trip to town. With a shrill voice she called Elsa to the parlor. Elsa ran downstairs and stopped in the doorway, surprised to see her mother's beaming face and the bulky package in her arms.

Eagerly Mother crossed the room and handed the parcel to Elsa. "We got it from a customer," she said. "Your nine dollars won't be quite enough, but your father and I will pay the difference."

Hesitantly Elsa took the package. It was wrapped in newspapers, stiff, wide at one end but narrow at the other. She could think of only one thing that had such a shape.

With trembling fingers she untied the string and tore off the layers of paper, scattering them on the floor. When the last paper fell free she was holding a battered, dark brown violin, its finish dull with age and laced with scratches. Timidly she twanged a string, stroked the wood, slid her hand along the fingerboard.

"Mine?" she asked softly.

Smiling, her mother nodded. "You're to have lessons too, from the new dentist's wife, and we've ordered a case from our wholesale house."

Elsa lifted the violin to her shoulder and nestled her chin into the cool hardness of the chin rest. She looked along the strings, past her fingers, past the pegs. At the end of the instrument instead of a curling scroll she saw a carved lion's head with open jaws. The lion seemed to smile back at her, encouraging her to try.

Awkwardly she laid the bow to a string and drew forth a scrunchy sound. "I can play it," she thought. "I

know I can." She stroked the string more lightly and heard a soft tone. "Now if I put down a finger I'll get another note," she thought. "I've watched just how they do it."

Shiny-eyed, her mother watched while Elsa experimented. She found two notes of a scale, then a third, and from those she built part of "Yankee Doodle." Long after her mother had left the room she struggled.

The next day she wrapped the violin again in newspaper to carry it to her first lesson. She soon found that playing took long, hard practice. But as the weeks passed into months, Elsa's skill grew. She became a fine player.

"Sorry, dear — we'll have to stop lessons for a while," her father would say when business was bad. Then she would practice by herself until times were better.

The teacher herself finally ended the lessons. "Elsa is too advanced for me," she explained.

"Where shall we take her?" Mother was worried.

"You might try Ted Gordon in Cedar City. He plays only wind instruments, but he has some violin pupils and gets good results. There isn't an expert string teacher anywhere close."

Mr. Gordon was a tall, spectacled man, alert, with quick movements and a wide grin. Elsa liked him at once, but his class was full.

"At least hear her play," begged Mother.

Mr. Gordon agreed, and sat quietly with his hands clasped. When Elsa finished he jumped up. "I'll take her. But she needs a better instrument."

"Someday," said mother, "when there's money. For now, lessons are all we can afford."

That fall they drove to Cedar City — and Mr. Gordon — every weekend. When drifting snows made the roads dangerous, Elsa made the trip by train.

Because Elsa was small for 13, her parents told her to buy a half-fare ticket, and each time the conductor came around she shrank trembling into her seat. One afternoon he looked closely at her.

"How old are you, young lady?" he asked.

"I'm — I'm — e — el — 13, sir," she faltered.

The moustache bristled as he looked from her to the ticket in his hand. "That's 40 cents more."

"Yes, sir." Her cheeks burned as she paid the difference, cringing at the conductor's loud voice.

All the way home she crouched in the corner of the

red plush seat, lurching with the train, staring through the window at the lonely landscape.

When she reached home and told what had happened, she burst into tears. Her mother was indignant.

"I don't think that conductor was one bit nice," she cried. "He needn't have been so cross."

Elsa's blue eyes flashed. "That's not the point! The railroad charges by age. It was cheating! We're always cheating!" she clenched her fist.

"Don't forget, all these lessons cost money," said her mother. "If we don't cut corners you can't take them."

Elsa covered her face, sobbing.

Her father patted her shoulder. "We can manage the extra money, dear. It won't happen again."

The year she was 14, Mr. Gordon asked for her help.

"Raymond Miles is to have a new violin for Christmas — a surprise," he said one day in November. "Don't you dare tell!"

"Not a soul." Elsa knew Raymond, a friendly boy whom she had once beaten in a contest.

"I have some violins here on trial, and I want to be sure Raymond gets the best. Would you help pick it out?" Mr. Gordon showed her three violins.

"First," he said, "play some scales. Warm up."

Elsa selected an instrument, laid it on her shoulder, and ran her fingers along the strings. She caught her breath as the notes tumbled from it. "If Raymond has one of these he might beat me in the next contest," she thought.

She tried another, then the third, and then played them all again. Soon she discovered that one violin seemed stiff. "Fast things are hard to play on this one," she thought. "I hope Raymond gets it. No, I don't — he should have the best — but with this he'd be easier to beat."

Mr. Gordon, she knew, only played wind instruments. As good a teacher as he was, he had no interest in playing the violin. So Elsa tried hard to play well on the stiff violin. "Sometimes it skips a quick note," she thought. "I won't play very fast. Maybe he won't notice."

"Which has the finest G string, Elsa?"

"Oh, this one." Holding the stiff instrument she played a few notes with all the resonance she could muster, thinking, "Of course Mr. Gordon will have someone else play them too." She switched to another, still thinking, "For myself, I'd want this light-colored one that plays like the wind."

When the test was finished Mr. Gordon held the stiff violin and looked at it doubtfully. "You picked this one every time, Elsa." He turned it over and continued, "It does have a beautiful tone, but is it flexible? That is important too." He laid his hand on the light-colored instrument. "This other also sounds beautiful, and you seemed to play it with more ease. Are you quite sure?"

"Quite." She looked down at the violins.

"Well, then, how shall we mark it?" He walked toward a table which was littered with his wife's sewing. "How about this red thread? Red for Christmas!" After tying a thread around one peg, he proceeded with the rest of the lesson.

Elsa played badly. "I've cheated again," she thought. "And cheating Raymond is worse than the railroad. A big company wouldn't notice the difference. But a violin means so much."

She tried to tell her teacher. "Mr. Gordon. There's something — "

"Yes, Elsa?"

"Never mind."

All the weeks before Christmas the thought of Raymond and his violin troubled Elsa. She helped string popcorn for the tree. She decorated special cookies. She tried to match her family's gaiety.

"You didn't tell us what you want this year," said her father. "Not a doll, I hope!"

"No — not a doll," Elsa answered. She thought of Raymond's violin and sighed.

Christmas Eve, as always, they burned their tongues on oyster stew and then hurried to church. Afterward everyone tramped home through the snow and merrily hung a stocking.

It snowed in the night, so the morning was clear and bright. The base of the Christmas tree was hidden by a drift of packages tied with crimson bows. Colored lights glowed among the popcorn and cranberries. Susan and Freddie squealed with excitement.

"See, Susan." That was Aunt Laura. "See what Santa left you! A ma-ma doll! Bend it over." Aunt Laura held the doll for a wondering Susan.

"There are mittens, mittens all 'round." That was Mother, who had knit them late at night.

"And what have you, Elsa?" This from Father. "Boots? And some books? But I see another package!"

Seeing the twinkle in her father's eyes, Elsa glanced warily where he pointed, and spied a large package, half hidden behind the others. Could it be the new coat she needed so badly?

The grown-ups quieted their cheerful hubbub to watch Elsa open her package. She sat down on the floor beside it and tore off the white paper. As she expected, the box was from Lampman's clothing store — probably the blue coat that had been in their window on sale.

Then she snatched off the cover and saw what the box contained — a violin. A violin, yes. But just one of Father's Christmas jokes. A cruel joke this time. It was

the battered dark fiddle with the lion's head scroll. Elsa turned away, clenching her hands, while the family shrieked with laughter.

"I guess we fooled you that time," Father spluttered. "Your old violin, in a Lampman's coat box." His shoulders were shaking, but when he noticed her quivering lips he added gently, "Elsa — old Santa isn't such a bad sort. Why don't you look in your violin case?"

She jumped up, scurried across the room, snatched her case from the corner and laid it on the table. With trembling fingers she fumbled at the catch and lifted out a violin. It was shiny and new and looked very familiar. But Elsa, running her hand up to the pegs, found, as she had somehow expected, a little piece of red thread!

"How shall we mark it?" Mr. Gordon had said. And he had tied that red thread to the stiff violin Elsa had chosen for Raymond.

"Red is for Christmas," she thought now. "But Mr. Gordon picked the wrong color. He should have chosen green — for envy." Silently she stroked the strings, imagining how it would have felt to own the light-colored violin.

As she glanced at her parents' beaming faces she suddenly remembered that her father had decided to wear his threadbare overcoat for another winter and that her mother had spent hours beside the window making over an old dress. Gently putting the violin back into its case, she rushed to her father.

He patted her shoulder. "How about a tune, Elsa?"

"Your favorite?" He nodded his head.

As she picked up the violin the red thread dangled limp, its knot half untied. Slowly and carefully, Elsa took the ends of the thread in her fingers. And firmly she retied the knot. Then laying bow to string she quickly tuned her instrument and played — not too fast — while her family joyously sang:

"We wish you a Merry Christmas,
We wish you a Merry Christmas,
We wish you a Merry Christmas,
And a Happy New Year."

Dorothy N. Morrison

PERFECT PRESENT

If you're looking for something un-usual to send
As a present this Christmas to some good old friend,
I think you will find that an excellent gift
Is a Fluff-footed, Frizzle-topped, Three-fingered Zifft.

A fine gift to give in all gift giving seasons,
He makes a fine present for twenty-three reasons.
The first reason is: He won't talk in his sleep.
The second one is that his food is quite cheap.
The third reason is: If you go anywhere
You can take him along on the train for half fare.
The fourth reason is: He is a friendly with eagles
And won't pick a fight with your neighborhood beagles.
The fifth reason is: When you talk on the phone
He won't make a racket or blow a trombone.
The sixth reason is that this wonderful pet
Doesn't smell terribly bad when he's wet
And the rest of the reasons I sort of forget,
But I certainly *do* recommend as a gift
The Fluff-footed, Frizzle-topped, Three-fingered Zifft.

Dr. Seuss

The Christmas Foundling

Angus Griggs was walking home with his son Jamie the night they saw it thrown in the river. It was the 23rd of December, after ten o'clock, and a fine drizzle was falling on the little village in Scotland. A car swooshed past them and stopped in the middle of the stone bridge. Next they saw a man haul out of the car something that looked like a heavy sack, and push it over the railing. Then the car drove off, the rear lights dwindling to two red dots.

In a flash, Angus and Jamie were up on the bridge peering down into the swirling water thirty feet below.

Jamie was the first to sight it. "There 'tis!"

"Where, Jamie? Where?"

"Down there by the arch! That black bubble — where the current spins!"

Angus stared through the blackness. "Thought I saw it! But truth, it's gone again!"

"It keeps sinking, then bobbing up again. Dadda! I think it's alive! Oh! Now the current has it! Look at it start to go!"

"*Now* I see it! It's a dog! The poor thing will be over the falls next!"

"Those fearsome rocks at the bottom!" Jamie moaned. "Oh, what can we do to save him?"

"There's naught we *can* do, lad. If I could swim I'd be after him in a minute, but without a boat or a net it's no use. Come home, Jamie. It doesn't bear watching."

Trying to draw the boy away, Angus started again along the bridge. After a few paces he looked round and saw Jamie out of his cap, jacket, and boots, climbing over the railings. "Stop, Jamie! Stop!" Angus shouted, dashing to make a grab for him. But Jamie was gone — feet first — plummeting down into the rushing darkness. Angus heard the water hit Jamie's body a great thwack, and as it closed over his head, he could almost see Jamie turn stiff from the shock and terrible cold.

"Catch hold of the arch!" Angus yelled, as gasping and choking, Jamie surfaced. There was no answer. Like the animal before him, Jamie spun in the icy current, unable to find his muscles.

"Did ye hear me, Jamie?" his father shouted again. "Hold to the bridge! I'll run and get ye a rope!"

But Jamie didn't hear or didn't heed. He must have found his muscles, for now he struck off downstream.

Farther down the river, Angus could still make out the small blob of the dog's head, disappearing, reappearing, and swerving from side to side; not swimming the way any sensible animal would swim.

The bridge was deserted. His heart pounding, Angus raced to the bank toward which he knew the current turned. Sliding down the muddy bank, he scrambled over the slippery rocks along the edge of the river, calling

"Jamie! Jamie! Where are ye? Give over lad! Swim for the shore!" Through the rain and the wind he thought he heard an answering call. But it was hard to tell, for now the noise of the falls was growing louder.

Shouting himself hoarse, Angus waded into the river. It was then he heard Jamie's faint voice call, "I have him!" Half wading, half climbing over the boulders, Angus tried to keep abreast of the sound of the swimmers. It seemed an age before they came in view — Jamie had one hand on the scruff of the dog's neck, while with his free arm and legs he was struggling feebly, ever more feebly, toward the shore.

"Here I am, Jamie!" Reaching out as far as he dared, Angus was able to seize hold of Jamie's outstretched fingers. He leaned backwards and gave a mighty pull. With that, the dog's wet neck slipped from the boy's tired grasp, and Angus saw the animal, with its terrified, stricken eyes, being borne away down the stream!

Gasping, sobbing, Jamie flung himself on the rocks, his cries of, "He's gone! He's gone!" muffled by the roar of the nearby falls.

"Ye had courage, lad! No one could have tried harder," Angus said, his face in his hands.

When he looked up again, he could hardly believe his eyes. The dog was still alive! Only a few yards from shore, its neck extended, its back braced against the murky sky, it was crouched in the water on the flat top of the concrete dam. Something had caught and trapped it there.

Shaking with cold and fear, Angus clambered over the

rocks up alongside. Then back into the river he went. One false move and over the falls he would go! His fingers clutched the rough inner edge of the dam as he slithered sideways, water foaming about his shoulders. The next minute he had found it — the short piece of rope, one end around the outstretched neck, the other end attached to a lead weight, and the weight snagged in the roots of a fallen tree. With a jerk, Angus dislodged the weight and, holding the rope taut, he inched himself and the dog toward the bank. At long last they toppled onto the shore, shivering with cold.

An instant later Jamie was beside him, his teeth chattering.

Side by side the three of them, stumbling against each other in the darkness, crawled up the steep bank to the lighted street. The sight of the holiday shop windows reminded Jamie:

"The Christmas cookies in m'pockets are all a moosh. Mother said I was to give ye some. Will she be letting us keep the beastie, d'ye think?"

"I was wondering just that, lad. Your mother is ..." Angus sighed. "When I was growing, I always had a dog, but your mother doesn't favor animals. She's had no experience with them. Her family never had so much as a bird."

"It will break m'heart if she doesn't!"

"Then let me handle it, Jamie," Angus said, "perhaps I can win her round."

A few minutes later, Angus pushed opened the door of

their cottage. Maggie Griggs looked up from the rocker where she sat knitting by a coal fire.

"Saints above! Whatever have the pair of ye been up to?" Maggie sprang to her feet. "Did ye push one another in the river? Jamie! Where's your jacket? And no *boots*!"

"Down on the bridge, and his cap too." Angus spoke between blue lips.

"Ye'll catch your death!" She rapped her knuckles against the staircase. "David! Wake up! I want ye to fetch your brother's clothes." She turned back to them. "Hold still and let me undo the buttons."

"Undo Jamie's; not mine awhile. First, I've brought a friend to make your acquaintance."

"At this hour!" Maggie's hand flew to her neat hair, her eyes searching the neat room.

Four heads of assorted sizes peered over the banister. "Are ye all called David?" scolded their mother. "Back to bed with the rest of ye!"

"Jamie! What happened?" they chorused. And then, "Ooh, look at that!" as Angus with the great black dog lumbered into the room.

"It's Jamie's Christmas present," said Angus. "A day or two ahead of time, but welcome."

"Speak for yourself, Angus Griggs," said his wife. "No great hungry beast is welcomed by me!

"I'm thinking a boy has a right to a Christmas present he's risked his life for!" said Angus gently. "'Twas a brave act on his part."

The children tumbled down the stairs. "Was he drowned, Jamie?" "How did ye save him?"

"Faith! I shall lose m'wits!" cried Maggie. "All this hubbub, and water all over m'clean floor! Into the kitchen with the three of ye, and off with your things. As for ye, David, down to the bridge on the double and find your brother's clothes before somebody thieves them."

Angus and Jamie were soon sitting by the fire, wrapped in woolen blankets, mugs of sweet steaming tea cupped in their hands. Between them lay the great black dog, the children taking turns drying its fur.

"He can sleep the night in the kitchen," announced Mrs. Griggs, "but tomorrow we look for his owner."

"A body who throws a dog in the river with a weight around its neck isn't worthy to be called an owner!" stated Angus. "That's m'opinion!"

"Please let him stay, Mother!" "We love him already," the children cried.

"Look at his poor neck where the rope's cut it," mourned Jamie. "How can folks be so cruel?"

"Fetch our guest a bowl of warm soup, Agnes," said her father. "It fair turns m'stomach to be sitting here enjoying m'tea with the poor creature likely as not half-starved."

"What shall we call him, Dadda?" little Alice asked.

"I've a *wonderful* idea!" said Sheila. "Let's call him Jingle. It has a Christmas sound!"

"No Sheila," Angus replied. "We will not be calling it Jingle. Jingle was m'first dog and the best dog I ever had. Every dog has a right to its own name."

"Then we must be after thinking of a good *new* name," Agnes said.

"Wouldn't the creature feel more at home to be called by its *own* name?" Angus asked.

"How can we tell, Dadda? It has no collar!"

"If it's an educated dog it'll tell us itself. Put another lump of coal on the fire, and . . ."

"Do you know what *time* it is, Angus Griggs?"

"Yes, Maggie; thinking time and Christmas time."

The door of the cottage blew open. David had returned with his brother's clothes.

"Come quickly, David," Jamie called. "We're asking the dog his name! It's a great sport."

The children crowded closer. "Let's begin!"

"All right! Everybody quiet now!" Leaning forward, Angus fixed the dog with his eyes. "A, B," he said. "Uh, Buh. C, D. Suh, Duh." Puzzled, polite, the dog gazed back as Angus sounded slowly through the alphabet. "P, Q. Pea, Cue." The great dog pricked its ears. "Ah, we're growing closer now. Everybody think! P, Q." The dog laughed and thumped its tail.

"I never heard of such a daft name!" said Maggie. "P Q P Q P!" The dog jumped up and spun in a circle. "I have it! I have it!" she cried. "It's Cupid! Cupid, of course!"

"Maggie! You're the clever one!" said Angus.

Mrs. Griggs flushed with pleasure. The dog, its eyes shining, licked her hand.

"Well, I never!" Maggie exclaimed, staring at her hand. "Still, it *is* a daft name for such a great beast."

"T'wasn't so daft when it was a round ball of black fur," Angus retorted. "And considering that Cupid was the wee god of love, ye might call it a very good name indeed."

"What's ailing him now?" Maggie broke in. She eyed the animal as it ran round and round the room, sniffing at the corners. Suddenly it began to whine and bite at itself. "Quick, David! Open the door. Perhaps he's wanting to go out!"

"Fetch us the laundry basket, lad," said Angus. "It isn't out she's wanting, Maggie. It's a bed and a dark corner."

"*She!*" Maggie looked stunned.

"Where are your eyes, girl? Can't you see Cupid's about to become a mother? That's why they threw her over the bridge!"

"Oh!" cried Maggie. "Now that was a frightsome thing to do." She looked at the ring of pleading faces surrounding her. "Upstairs with the pack of ye!" she cried. "And don't be disturbing the patient. Your father and I may have something to show ye in the morning."

"A Christmas present for each of the kiddies if I know anything," Angus said to himself. "Give her time, lad," he whispered to Jamie. "Your mother has to be led on a loose rein."

Mrs. Griggs herded the children up the stairs.

"There should have been a dog in the stable," spoke Jamie, bringing up the rear.

"No more chatter! Up to bed with ye!" commanded Maggie. "*What* stable?"

"The holy stable. The ox and donkey are very nice, but a dog is a *truly* lovesome thing."

"Maybe so, said Maggie. "But I see no room in this house for a dog for very long."

"Have ye forgotten, Maggie," Angus asked quietly, "that there was no room at the Inn?"

Of a sudden, Maggie's eyes stood still, then a tear, brighter than a moonstone, trickled slowly down her cheek.

She turned to the staircase. "Jamie? Jamie boy," she called softly, "throw me down m'red quilt. I'm thinking of making Cupid a welcome Christmas crib."

Margaret W. Tuttle

DECEMBER

I like days
with a snow-white collar,
and nights when the moon
is a silver dollar,
and hills are filled
with eiderdown stuffing
and your breath makes smoke
like an engine puffing.

I like days
when feathers are snowing,
and all the eaves
have petticoats showing,
and the air is cold,
and wires are humming,
but you feel all warm . . .
with Christmas coming!

Aileen Fisher

The Christmas Horses

Thanksgiving was past and it was time to think of Christmas. Still there was no snow and no rain. The sky was gray, the prairie was dull, and the winds were cold. But the cold winds blew over the top of the dugout.

Laura and Mary knew that Santa Claus could not come down a chimney when there was no chimney.

One day Mary asked Ma how Santa Claus could come. Ma did not answer. Instead, she asked, "What do you girls want for Christmas?"

She was ironing. One end of the ironing board was on the table and the other on the bedstead. Pa had made the bedstead that high, on purpose. Carrie was playing on the bed and Laura and Mary sat at the table. Mary was sorting quilt blocks and Laura was making a little apron for the rag doll, Charlotte. The wind howled overhead and whined in the stovepipe, but there was no snow yet.

Laura said, "I want candy."

"So do I," said Mary, and Carrie cried, "Tandy?"

"And a new winter dress, and a coat, and a hood," said Mary.

"So do I," said Laura. "And a dress for Charlotte, and — "

Ma lifted the iron from the stove and held it out to them. They could test the iron. They licked their fingers and touched them, quicker than quick, to the smooth hot bottom. If it crackled, the iron was hot enough.

"Thank you, Mary and Laura," Ma said. She began carefully ironing around and over the patches on Pa's shirt. "Do you know what Pa wants for Christmas?"

They did not know.

"Horses," Ma said. "Would you girls like horses?"

Laura and Mary looked at each other.

"I only thought," Ma went on, "if we all wished for horses, and nothing but horses, then maybe — "

Laura felt queer. Horses were everyday; they were not Christmas. If Pa got horses, he would trade for them. Laura could not think of Santa Claus and horses at the same time.

"Ma!" she cried. "There *is* a Santa Claus, isn't there?"

"Of course there's a Santa Claus," said Ma. She set the iron on the stove to heat again.

"The older you are, the more you know about Santa Claus," she said. "You are so big now, you know he can't be just one man, don't you? You know he is everywhere on Christmas Eve. He is in the Big Woods, and in Indian Territory, and far away in York State, and here. He comes down all the chimneys at the same time. You know that, don't you?"

"Yes, Ma," said Mary and Laura.

"Well," said Ma. "Then you see — "

"I guess he is like angels," Mary said, slowly. And Laura could see that, just as well as Mary could.

Then Ma told them something else about Santa Claus. He was everywhere, and besides that, he was all the time.

Wherever anyone was unselfish, that was Santa Claus.

Christmas Eve was the time when everybody was unselfish. On that one night, Santa Claus was everywhere, because everybody, all together, stopped being selfish and wanted other people to be happy. And in the morning you saw what that had done.

"If everybody wanted everybody else to be happy, all the time, then would it be Christmas all the time?" Laura asked, and Ma said, "Yes, Laura."

Laura thought about that. So did Mary. They thought, and they looked at each other, and they knew what Ma wanted them to do. She wanted them to wish for nothing but horses for Pa. They looked at each other again and they looked away quickly and they did not say anything. Even Mary, who was always so good, did not say a word.

That night after supper Pa drew Laura and Mary close to him in the crook of his arms. Laura looked up at his face, and then she snuggled against him and said, "Pa."

"What is it, little half-pint of sweet cider?" Pa asked, and Laura said:

"Pa, I want Santa Claus — to bring — "

"What?" Pa asked.

"Horses," said Laura. "If you will let me ride them sometimes."

"So do I!" said Mary. But Laura had said it first.

Pa was surprised. His eyes shone soft and bright at them. "Would you girls really like horses?" he asked them.

"Oh yes, Pa!" they said.

"In that case," said Pa, smiling, "I have an idea that Santa Claus will bring us all a fine team of horses."

That settled it. They would not have any Christmas, only horses. Laura and Mary soberly undressed and soberly buttoned up their nightgowns and tied their nightcap strings. They knelt down together and said,

> "Now I lay me down to sleep,
> I pray the Lord my soul to keep.
> If I should die before I wake
> I pray the Lord my soul to take,

and please bless Pa and Ma and Carrie and everybody and make me a good girl for ever'n'ever. Amen."

Quickly Laura added, in her own head, "And please make me only glad about the Christmas horses, for ever'n'ever amen again."

She climbed into bed and almost right away she was glad. She thought of horses sleek and shining, of how their manes and tails blew in the wind, how they picked up their swift feet and sniffed the air with velvety noses and looked at everything with bright, soft eyes. And Pa would let her ride them.

Pa had tuned his fiddle and now he set it against his shoulder. Overhead the wind went wailing lonely in the cold dark. But in the dugout everything was snug and cozy.

Bits of firelight came through the seams of the stove and twinkled on Ma's steel knitting-needles and tried to catch Pa's elbow. In the shadows the bow was dancing, on the floor Pa's toe was tapping, and the merry music hid the lonely crying of the wind.

Next morning, snow was in the air. Hard bits of snow were leaping and whirling in the howling wind.

Laura could not go out to play. In the stable, Spot and Pete and Bright stood all day long, eating the hay and straw. In the dugout, Pa mended his boots while Ma read to him again the story called "Millbank." Mary sewed and Laura played with paper dolls. She could let Carrie hold Charlotte, but Carrie was too little to play with paper dolls; she might tear one.

That afternoon, when Carrie was asleep, Ma beckoned Mary and Laura. Her face was shining with a secret. They put their heads close to hers, and she told them. They could make a button-string for Carrie's Christmas!

They climbed onto their bed and turned their backs to Carrie and spread their laps wide. Ma brought them her button box.

The box was almost full. Ma had saved buttons since she was smaller than Laura, and she had buttons her mother had saved when her mother was a little girl. There were blue buttons and red buttons, silvery and goldy buttons, curved-in buttons with tiny raised castles and bridges and trees on them, and twinkling jet buttons, painted china buttons, striped buttons, buttons like juicy blackberries, and even one tiny dog-head button. Laura squealed when she saw it.

"Sh!" Ma shushed her. But Carrie did not wake up.

Ma gave them all those buttons to make a button-string for Carrie.

After that, Laura did not mind staying in the dugout. When she saw the outdoors, the wind was driving snow-drifts across the bare, frozen land. The creek was ice and the willow tops rattled. In the dugout she and Mary had their secret.

They played gently with Carrie and gave her every-thing she wanted. They cuddled her and sang to her and got her to sleep whenever they could. Then they worked on the button-string.

Mary had one end of the string and Laura had the other. They picked out the buttons they wanted and strung them on the string. They held the string out and looked at it, and took off some buttons and put on others. Sometimes they took every button off, and started again. They were going to make the most beautiful button-string in the world.

One day Ma told them that this was the day before Christmas. They must finish the button-string that day.

They could not get Carrie to sleep. She ran and shouted, climbed on benches and jumped off, and skipped and sang. She did not get tired. Mary told her to sit still like a little lady, but she wouldn't. Laura let her hold Charlotte, and she jounced Charlotte up and down and flung her against the wall.

Finally Ma cuddled her and sang. Laura and Mary were perfectly still. Lower and lower Ma sang, and Carrie's eyes blinked till they shut. When softly Ma stopped singing, Carrie's eyes popped open and she shouted, "More, Ma! More!"

But at last she fell asleep. Then quickly, quickly, Laura and Mary finished the button-string. Ma tied the ends together for them. It was done; they could not change one button more. It was a beautiful button-string.

That evening after supper, when Carrie was sound asleep, Ma hung her clean little pair of stockings from the table edge. Laura and Mary, in their nightgowns, slid the button-string into one stocking.

Then that was all. Mary and Laura were going to bed when Pa asked them, "Aren't you girls going to hang your stockings?"

"But I thought," Laura said, "I thought Santa Claus was going to bring us horses."

"Maybe he will," said Pa. "But little girls always hang up their stockings on Christmas Eve, don't they?"

Laura did not know what to think. Neither did Mary. Ma took two clean stockings out of the clothes box, and Pa helped hang them beside Carrie's. Laura and Mary said their prayers and went to sleep, wondering.

In the morning Laura heard the fire crackling. She opened one eye the least bit, and saw lamplight, and a bulge in her Christmas stocking.

She yelled and jumped out of bed. Mary came running too, and Carrie woke up. In Laura's stocking, and in Mary's stocking, there were little paper packages, just alike. In the packages was candy.

Laura had six pieces, and Mary had six. They had never

seen such beautiful candy. It was too beautiful to eat. Some pieces were like ribbons, bent in waves. Some were short bits of round stick candy, and on their flat ends were colored flowers that went all the way through. Some were perfectly round and striped.

In one of Carrie's stockings were four pieces of that beautiful candy. In the other was the button-string. Carrie's eyes and her mouth were perfectly round when she saw it. Then she squealed, and grabbed it and squealed again. She sat on Pa's knee, looking at her candy and her button-string and wriggling and laughing with joy.

Then it was time for Pa to do the chores. He said, "Do you suppose there is anything for us in the stable?" And Ma said, "Dress as fast as you can, girls, and you can go to the stable and see what Pa finds."

It was winter, so they had to put on stockings and shoes. But Ma helped them button up the shoes and she pinned their shawls under their chins. They ran out into the cold.

Everything was gray, except a long red streak in the eastern sky. Its red light shone on the patches of gray-white snow. Snow was caught in the dead grass on the walls and roof of the stable and it was red. Pa stood waiting in the stable door. He laughed when he saw Laura and Mary, and he stepped outside to let them go in.

There, standing in Pete's and Bright's places, were two horses.

They were larger than Pet and Patty, and they were a soft, red-brown color, shining like silk. Their manes and tails were black. Their eyes were bright and gentle. They put their velvety noses down to Laura and nibbled softly at her hand and breathed warm on it.

"Well, flutterbudget!" said Pa, "and Mary. How do you girls like your Christmas?"

"Very much, Pa," said Mary, but Laura could only say, "Oh Pa!"

Pa's eyes shone deep and he asked, "Who wants to ride the Christmas horses to water?"

Laura could hardly wait while he lifted Mary up and showed her how to hold on to the mane, and told her not to be afraid. Then Pa's strong hands swung Laura up. She

sat on the horse's big, gentle back and felt its aliveness carrying her.

All outdoors was glittering now with sunshine on snow and frost. Pa went ahead, leading the horses and carrying his ax to break the ice in the creek so they could drink. The horses lifted their heads and took deep breaths and whooshed the cold out of their noses. Their velvety ears pricked forward, then back and forward again.

Laura held to her horse's mane and clapped her shoes together and laughed. Pa and the horses and Mary and Laura were all happy in the gay, cold Christmas morning.

Laura Ingalls Wilder

BABOUSHKA

On the night when the Christ Child was born in Bethlehem, in a country far away, an old, old woman named Baboushka sat in her snug little house by her warm fire. The wind was drifting the snow outside and howling down the chimney, but it only made Baboushka's fire burn more brightly.

"How glad I am that I may stay indoors!" said Baboushka, holding her hands out to the bright blaze.

But suddenly she heard a loud rap at the door. She opened it and her candle shone on three old men standing outside in the snow. Their beards were as white as snow, and so long they reached to the ground. Their eyes shone kindly in the light of Baboushka's candle, and their arms were full of precious things — boxes of jewels, and sweet-smelling oils, and ointments.

"We have traveled far, Baboushka," they said, "and we

stop to tell you of the Baby born this night in Bethlehem. He comes to rule the world and teach all men to be loving and true. We carry gifts to Him. Come with us, Baboushka!"

But Baboushka looked at the driving snow, and then inside at her cozy room and the crackling fire. "It is too late for me to go with you, good sirs," she said. "The weather is too cold." She went inside again and shut the door, and the old men journeyed on to Bethlehem without her. But as Baboushka sat by her fire, rocking, she began to think about the little Christ Child, for she loved all babies.

"Tomorrow I will go to find Him," she said, "tomorrow, when it is light, and I will carry Him some toys."

So when it was morning, Baboushka put on her long cloak and took her staff and filled a basket with the pretty things a baby would like — gold balls, and wooden toys, and strings of silver cobwebs — and she set out to find the Christ Child.

But Baboushka had forgotten to ask the three old men the road to Bethlehem, and they had traveled so far through the night that she could not overtake them. Up and down the roads she hurried, through woods and fields and towns, saying to whoever she met: "I am looking for the Christ Child. Where does He lie? I have some pretty toys for Him."

But no one could tell her the way to go, and they all said: "Farther on, Baboushka, farther on." So she traveled on, and on, and on for years and years, but she never found the little Christ Child.

They say the old Baboushka is traveling still, looking for Him. When Christmas Eve comes, and the children are lying fast asleep, Baboushka walks softly through the snowy fields and towns, wrapped in her long cloak and carrying her basket on her arms. With her staff she raps gently at the doors and goes inside and holds her candle close to the little children's faces.

"Is He here?" she asks. "Is the little Christ Child here?" And then she turns sorrowfully away again, crying: "Farther on, farther on."

But before she leaves, she takes a toy from her basket and lays it beside the pillow for a Christmas gift. "For His sake," she says softly.

And then she hurries on through the years and forever, in search of the little Christ Child.

Traditional

CITY CHRISTMAS

I will go walking in our town
   Now that it's Christmastime
To see the streets of shops all decked
   Gay as a pantomime.
There will be trinkets and toys galore,
   Candles for every tree
Stacked at the curb in spicy green
   Bristling needle-y.
There will be children with dimes to spend;
   Stars in the queerest places;
Lights that twinkle and lights that glow,
   And lights in people's faces.
I will go walking in our town,
   Knowing that all is well —
Seeing the sights of Christmas,
   Smelling each Christmas smell.

Rachel Field

A Christmas Tree for Lydia

Lydia first learned about Christmas when she was one year old. Draped over her mother's shoulder she drooled and stared and the lights of the Christmas tree made other lights in her large entranced eyes.

When she was two years old she learned about Santa Claus. She paid very little attention to him then, but when she was three she talked about him a lot and they had difficulty persuading her that he and the infant Jesus were not father and son. By the time she was four she had come to accept him as one of the ordered phenomena[1] that ruled her life, like daytime and night time: one seven o'clock for getting up and another seven o'clock for going to bed. Like praise and blame; winter and summer; and her brother's right to seniority and her mother's last word. Her father did not exist in her field of magnitudes[2]; he had been killed in Cassino the winter she was born.

"Santa Claus will come," Lydia said and knew it was as true as saying tomorrow will come. "He will bring a Christmas tree. Big. With lights. With colors."

1 facts   2 considerations

When she was four her brother Eddy was nine and had long ago found out the truth concerning the matter. No speck of illusion was in his eye when he passed the street-corner Santas at Christmastime, standing beside their imitation chimneys, ringing their bells. He saw them for what they were. He saw how all their trousers bagged and their sleeves were too long, and how, above the false beards tied on loosely like bibs, their noses ran and their eyes looked melancholy[3].

"You'd think the kid would catch on," Eddy said to his mother one day after he'd taken a walk with Lydia. "Gee, when you notice the differentness of them all."

Lydia believed in every one of them, from the bell-ringers on the street corners to the department-store variety who always asked the same questions and whose hired joviality[4] grew glassy toward evening. For Lydia the saint was everywhere, ingenious, capable of all; and, looking into the different faces of his impersonators[5], she beheld the one good face she had invented for him.

"Eddy, don't you tell her, now, will you?" his mother said. "Don't you dare to, now. Remember she's only four."

Sure, let the kid have her fun, thought Eddy, with large scorn and slight compassion[6]. He himself remembered long ago Christmas Eves when he had listened for bells in the air and watched the limp shape of his sock hung up over the stove.

"How can he come in through the *stove,* Mum?"

"In houses like this he comes in through the window. Go to sleep now, Eddy."

3 sad   4 jollity   5 imitators   6 kindness

Eddy went to public school in the daytime and Lydia went to a day nursery. Her mother called for her every evening on her way home from work. She was a thin dark young woman whose prettiness was often obscured[7] by the ragged shadows of irritation and fatigue. She loved her children but worry gnawed at her relations with them, sharpening her words and shortening her temper. Coming home in the evening, climbing up the stairs to the flat with one hand pressing the bags of groceries to her chest and Lydia loitering and babbling, dragging on her other hand, she wished sometimes to let go of everything. To let go of Lydia; to let go, once and for all, of all the heavy paper bags. It would be a savage happiness, she felt, to see and hear the ketchup bottle smashed on the stairs, the eggs broken and leaking, and all the tin cans and potatoes rolling and banging their way downward, downward.

They lived in a two-room flat with linoleum on the floor and a corrugated ceiling. In the daytime, from noon on, the rooms were hot with sunshine but in the morning and at night they were as cold as caves unless the stove was going. The stove and the bathtub would gulp lonesomely and the leaky tap of the sink had a drip as perfect in tempo as a clock. And sometimes a great storming and rumbling rose in the pipes, as though they were releasing a river genie.

Lydia and her mother slept in the back room, a darkish place, painted blue, with a big dim mirror over the bureau and a window looking onto an air shaft.

Eddy was often alone during the first part of his vaca-

7 hidden

tion. At noon, wearing his blue and gray mackinaw coat and his aviator's helmet with the straps flying, he came stamping up the stairs and into the sun-flooded crowded little flat. Humming and snuffling, he made his lunch: breakfast food, or huge erratic sandwiches filled with curious ingredients.

When he was through he always cleaned up: washed the bowl or dish and swept up the bread crumbs with his chapped hand. He had learned to be tidy at an early age and could even make his bed well enough to sleep in it.

In the afternoons and mornings he voyaged forth with Joey Camarda, and others, to the street for contests of skill and wit. Sometimes they went to the upper reaches of the park with its lakes, bridges, battlegrounds, and ambushes. On rainy days they tagged through the museums, shrill and shabby as sparrows, touching the raddled surfaces of meteorites without awe and tipping back their heads boldly to stare at the furious mask of Tyrannosaurus rex.

"He isn't real. They made him out of pieces of wood, like," Joey said. "Men with ladders made him."

"He is too, real," Eddy said. "He walked around and ate and growled and everything. Once he did."

"Naw, he wasn't real. He couldn't be real. You'd believe anything. You'd believe in Santa Claus even."

Christmas and its symbols were more and more in their conversation as the time drew near. They speculated[8] on the subject of possible gifts to themselves. Joey said his uncle was going to give him roller skates and a rifle.

Eddy said he thought he'd probably get a bike. It was

8 thought

just as likely he would be given a bike as that he would be given the new moon out of the sky, but having made the statement he went on to perfect it. He said that it would be a white bike with red trimming and a piece of red glass like a jewel on the back of it and two raccoon tails floating from the handle bars.

"There's going to be two kinds of bells on the handle bars. One will be kind of a siren."

"Will you let me ride on it sometimes, Ed?"

"Sometimes," Eddy said.

That night he rode the dream bike all around the flat with the raccoon tails flying out on the speed-torn air. The tail light blazed like a red-hot ruby and the siren was as terrible as human voice could make it.

"Watch me now, I'm taking a curve," shouted Eddy. "Eee-ow-oooo-eee. Just missed that truck by a half an inch."

Lydia sat safely on the bed in the back room questioning him as he flashed by.

"Is it a plane, Eddy?"

"No."

"Is it a car?"

"No."

"Is it a — is it a train?"

"No. Gosh, it's a bike. Look out now, I got to make that light. Eee-ow-oo-ee!"

"Eddy, will you please for pity's sake *shut up!*" cried his mother. "I can't even hear myself think!"

He came to a stop in the doorway. "Gee, Mum, what are you so cross about?"

She didn't look at him; she pushed the potatoes and onions around the frying pan with a fork. Then she shook salt over them and spoke as if from a great distance.

"Close the door. Eddy, you kids don't get a tree this year."

"Heck, why not? What did we do?"

"I can't afford it, that's why," she said loudly, angry with him because she was hurting him. Then she lowered her voice. "They don't want me back at the store after Christmas. They told me today. They don't need me any more. I can't get you any presents but just things you have to have like socks and mittens." She looked at him. "Maybe some candy," she added.

A stinging hot odor rose from the frying pan to join the robust company of cooking smells from other flats on other floors: herring and chili and garlic and pork.

"Gee, Eddy, I'm scared to spend another cent. How do I know I'll get another job very soon?"

"What are you going to tell Lydia? She talks about the Christmas tree all day long."

"She'll have to do without one, that's all. Other people have to do without."

"But, gee, she talks about it all day long."

His mother threw down the fork and whirled on him. "I can't *help* it, can I? Good heavens, what am *I* supposed to do?"

Eddy knew better than to go on with it. He leaned against the sink and thought and when they ate supper he was kind and forbearing[9] with Lydia, who was both hilarious and sloppy. After a while his kindness became

9 patient

preoccupied, like that of one who drinks secretly at a spring of inspiration, and when Lydia had gone to bed he made a suggestion to his mother.

"I have an idea. If we put Christmas off for a few days, maybe a week, I can fix everything."

His mother, as he had expected, said no. It was this response on the part of his mother which was the starting point of all his campaigns, many of them successful. He leaned against the sink and waited.

"What good would it do? And anyway what would Lydia think!" she said.

"Tell her Santa Claus is late. Tell her we made a mistake about the day. She's too dumb to know the difference. Everyone's dumb when they're four."

"And anyway it seems kind of wrong."

"What would Jesus care if we put His birthday off a couple of days?"

"Oh Eddy, don't be silly. There won't be any more money then than there is now."

"No, but I got an idea. Please, Mum, please. Please!"

Eddy knew how to pester nicely. He had a quiet attentive serious way of looking and looking at one; of following a person with his eyes and not saying anything, the request still shimmering all around him like heat lightning. He waited.

His mother hung up the wet dish towel and turned the dishpan upside down. She looked into the little mirror above the sink and looked away again. Then she sat down in the rocker and opened the newspaper.

"Oh, all *right*," she said. "For pity's sake, Eddy. What do you expect, a miracle?"

"Isn't there ever any miracles? Anyway I'm not thinking about a miracle, I'm thinking about something smart," Eddy said.

Christmas came, and for them it was a day like any other, except that their mother was at home. But it was easy to explain to Lydia that this was because her job at the store had ended for good, just as it was easy to explain Lydia's own absence from nursery school by the simple method of rubbing medicated cold salve on her chest. Eddy thought of that one too.

"Gee, Eddy, I hope you know what you're doing," his mother said.

"I do know," Eddy said.

"You should at least tell *me* what you're going to do."

"It has to be a surprise for you too," Eddy said not so much because he wanted to surprise his mother as because he knew if he revealed his plan he would come in contact with a "no" which none of his stratagems could dissolve.

"It will be okay, Mum."

"And when is it to be, if I may ask?"

"On New Year's Day, I guess," Eddy said and went in search of Joey Camarda, whose help he had enlisted.

On New Year's Eve, he shut Lydia and his mother into their room.

"No matter what noises you hear, you don't come out, see? Promise."

"Well —" his mother conceded[10] and that was as good as

10 admitted

promising. She went in and shut the door and before the extraordinary sounds of toil and shuffling commenced in the hall she was lost in the deep sleep of the discouraged: that brief time which is free from all the images of fear or joy.

At midnight the city woke up and met the New Year with a mighty purring. In the streets people blew horns and shook things that sounded like tin cans full of pebbles. Lydia woke up too and thought that it was Santa Claus.

"I wanna get up, Mum. I wanna see him."

"You lie down this minute or he won't leave a single thing. He doesn't like for people to be awake when he comes," said her mother crossly, clinging to the warm webs of sleep.

But Lydia sat up for a while in her cot, rocking softly to and fro. Through the crack under the door came a fragrance she remembered well from Christmas a year ago, and the Christmas before that.

In the morning it was a long time before Eddy would let them out of their room.

"Eddy, it's cold in here," said his mother.

"I wanna see the tree, I wanna see the tree," chanted Lydia, half singing, half whining. "I wanna see the tree, I wanna see the tree."

"Heck, wait a *minute*," said Eddy.

"I wanna see the tree, I wanna see the tree," bayed Lydia.

There were sounds of haste and struggle in the next room.

"All right you can come in now," said Eddy and opened the door.

They saw a forest.

In a circle, hiding every wall, stood the Christmas trees; spare ones and stout ones, tall ones and short ones, but all tall to Lydia. Some still were hung with threads of silver foil and here and there among the boughs, the Christmas ornaments for a single tree had been distributed; calm and bright as planets they turned and burned among the needles. The family stood in a mysterious grove, without bird or breeze, and there was a deep fragrance in the room. It was a smell of health and stillness and tranquility and for a minute or two, before she had thought of the dropping needles and the general inconvenience of a forest in the kitchen, Eddy's mother breathed the smell full into her city lungs and felt within herself a lessening of strain.

"Eddy, Eddy, how? How?"

"Me and Joe Camarda," Eddy whispered. "We went all around last night and dragged them out of gutters. We could of filled the whole entire house with them if we wanted to. Last night in here it was like camping out."

It had been like that. He had lain peacefully in his bed under the branches, listening to the occasional snowflake tinkle of a falling needle and to the ticking of the leaky tap, hidden now as any forest spring.

"Eddy honey, look at Lydia."

Lydia still looked new from her sleep. She stood with her hair rumpled and her eyes full of lights, and her hands clasped in front of her in a composed elderly way. Although she was naturally a loud exuberant child, the noise had temporarily been knocked out of her.

"All the Christmas trees," she said gently.

"Gee," said Eddy. "Don't get the idea it's going to be this way every year. This is just because he was late and it's instead of presents."

It was enough for Lydia, anyone could see that. In a way it was enough for Eddy too. He felt proud, generous and efficient. He felt successful. With his hands in his pockets he stood looking at his sister.

"All the Christmas trees," Lydia said quietly and sighed. "All the Christmas trees."

Elizabeth Enright

Illustrations by Peggy Fortnum.

Paddington's Christmas

Paddington found that Christmas took a long time to come. Each morning when he hurried downstairs he crossed the date off the calendar, but the more days he crossed off the farther away it seemed.

However, there was plenty to occupy his mind. For one thing, the postman started arriving later and later in the morning, and when he did finally reach the Browns' house there were so many letters to deliver he had a job to push them all through the letterbox. Often there were mysterious-looking parcels as well, which Mrs. Bird, the housekeeper, promptly hid before Paddington had time to squeeze them.

A surprising number of the envelopes were addressed to Paddington himself, and he carefully made a list of all those who had sent him Christmas cards so that he could be sure of thanking them.

"You may be only a small bear," said Mrs. Bird, as she

helped him arrange the cards on the mantelpiece, "but you certainly leave your mark."

Paddington wasn't sure how to take this, especially as Mrs. Bird had just polished the hall floor, but when he examined his paws they were quite clean.

Paddington had made his own Christmas cards. Some he had drawn himself, decorating the edges with holly and mistletoe; others had been made out of pictures cut from Mrs. Brown's magazines. But each one had the words "A Merry Christmas and a Happy New Year" printed on the front, and they were signed Padingtun Brown on the inside — together with his special paw mark to show that they were genuine.

Paddington wasn't sure about the spelling of "A Merry Christmas." It didn't look at all right. But Mrs. Bird checked all the words in a dictionary for him to make certain.

"I don't suppose many people get Christmas cards from a bear," she explained. "They'll probably want to keep them, so you ought to make sure they are right."

One evening Mr. Brown arrived home with a huge Christmas tree tied to the roof of his car. It was placed in a position of honor by the dining-room window and both Paddington and Mr. Brown spent a long time decorating it with colored lights and silver tinsel.

Apart from the Christmas tree, there were paper chains and holly to be put up, and large colored bells made of crinkly paper. Paddington enjoyed doing the paper chains. He managed to persuade Mr. Brown that bears were very good at putting up decorations and together they did most of the house, with Paddington standing on Mr. Brown's shoulders while Mr. Brown handed up the drawing pins. It came to an unhappy end one evening when Paddington accidentally put his paw on a drawing pin which he'd left on top of Mr. Brown's head. When Mrs. Bird rushed into the dining room to see what all the fuss was about, and to inquire why all the lights had suddenly gone out, she found Paddington hanging by his paws from the chandelier and Mr. Brown dancing around the room rubbing his head.

But by then the decorations were almost finished and the house had taken on quite a festive air. The sideboard was groaning under the weight of nuts and oranges, dates and figs, none of which Paddington was allowed to touch, and Mr. Brown had stopped smoking his pipe and was filling the air instead with the smell of cigars.

The excitement in the Browns' house mounted, until it reached fever pitch a few days before Christmas, when Jonathan and Judy arrived home for the holidays.

But if the days leading up to Christmas were busy and exciting, they were nothing compared with Christmas day itself.

The Browns were up early on Christmas morning — much earlier than they had intended. It all started when Paddington woke to find a large pillowcase at the bottom of his bed. His eyes nearly popped out with astonishment when he switched his torch on, for it was bulging with parcels, and it certainly hadn't been there when he'd gone to bed on Christmas Eve.

Paddington's eyes grew larger and larger as he unwrapped the brightly colored paper round each present. A few days before, on Mrs. Bird's instructions, he had made a list of all the things he hoped to have given him and had hidden it up one of the chimneys. It was a strange thing, but everything on that list seemed to be in the pillowcase.

There was a large chemistry set from Mr. Brown, full of jars and bottles and test tubes, which looked very interesting. And there was a miniature xylophone from Mrs. Brown, which pleased him no end. Paddington was fond of music — especially the loud sort, which was good for conducting — and he had always wanted something he could actually play.

Mrs. Bird's parcel was even more exciting, for it contained a checked cap which he'd specially asked for and had underlined on his list. Paddington stood on the end of his bed, admiring the effect in the mirror for quite a while.

Jonathan and Judy had each given him a travel book. Paddington was very interested in geography, being a much traveled bear, and he was pleased to see there were plenty of maps and colored pictures inside.

The noise from Paddington's room was soon sufficient to waken both Jonathan and Judy, and in no time at all the whole house was in an uproar, with wrapping paper and bits of string everywhere.

"I'm as patriotic as the next man," grumbled Mr. Brown. "But I draw the line when bears start playing the National Anthem at six o'clock in the morning — especially on a xylophone."

As always, it was left to Mrs. Bird to restore order. "No more presents until after lunch," she said, firmly. She had just tripped over Paddington on the upstairs landing, where he was investigating his new chemical outfit, and something nasty had gone in one of her slippers.

"It's all right, Mrs. Bird," said Paddington, consulting his instruction book, "it's only some iron filings. I don't think they're dangerous."

"Dangerous or not," said Mrs. Bird, "I've a big dinner to cook — not to mention your birthday cake to finish decorating."

Being a bear, Paddington had two birthdays each year — one in the summer and one at Christmas — and the Browns were holding a party in his honor to which Mr. Gruber had been invited.

After they'd had breakfast and been to church, the morning passed quickly and Paddington spent most of his time trying to decide what to do next. With so many things from which to choose it was most difficult. He read some chapters from his books and made several interesting smells and a small explosion with his chemical outfit.

Mr. Brown was already in trouble for having given it to

him, especially when Paddington found a chapter in the instruction book headed "Indoor Fireworks." He made himself a "never-ending" snake which wouldn't stop growing and frightened Mrs. Bird to death when she met it coming down the stairs.

"If we don't watch out," she confided to Mrs. Brown, "we shan't last over Christmas. We shall either be blown to smithereens or poisoned. He was testing my gravy with some litmus paper just now."

Mrs. Brown sighed. "It's a good job Christmas only comes once a year," she said, as she helped Mrs. Bird with the potatoes.

"It isn't over yet," warned Mrs. Bird.

Fortunately, Mr. Gruber arrived at that moment and some measure of order was established before they all sat down to dinner.

Paddington's eyes glistened as he surveyed the table. He didn't agree with Mr. Brown when he said it all looked too good to eat. All the same, even Paddington got noticeably slower toward the end when Mrs. Bird brought in the Christmas pudding.

"Well," said Mr. Gruber, a few minutes later, as he sat back and surveyed his empty plate, "I must say that's the best Christmas dinner I've had for many a day. Thank you very much indeed!"

"Hear! Hear!" agreed Mr. Brown. "What do you say, Paddington?"

"It was very nice," said Paddington, licking some cream from his whiskers. "Except I had a bone in my Christmas pudding."

"You *what?*" exclaimed Mrs. Brown. "Don't be silly — there are no bones in Christmas pudding."

"I had one," said Paddington, firmly. "It was all hard — and it stuck in my throat."

"Good gracious!" exclaimed Mrs. Bird. "The sixpence! I always put a piece of silver in the Christmas pudding."

"What!" said Paddington, nearly falling off his chair. "A sixpence? I've never heard of a sixpence pudding before."

"Quick," shouted Mr. Brown, rising to the emergency. "Turn him upside-down."

Before Paddington could reply, he found himself hanging head downwards while Mr. Brown and Mr. Gruber took turns to shake him. The rest of the family stood round watching the floor.

"It's no good," said Mr. Brown, after a while. "It must have gone too far." He helped Mr. Gruber lift Paddington into an armchair, where he lay gasping for breath.

"I've got a magnet upstairs," said Jonathan. "We could try lowering it down his throat on a piece of string."

"I don't think so, dear," said Mrs. Brown, in a worried tone of voice. "He might swallow that and then we should be even worse off." She bent over the chair. "How do you feel, Paddington?"

"Sick," said Paddington, in an aggrieved tone of voice.

"Of course you do, dear," said Mrs. Brown. "It's only to be expected. There's only one thing to do — we shall have to send for the doctor."

"Thank goodness I scrubbed it first," said Mrs. Bird. "It might have been covered with germs."

"But I *didn't* swallow it," gasped Paddington. "I only nearly did. Then I put it on the side of my plate. I didn't know it was a sixpence because it was all covered with Christmas pudding."

Paddington felt very fed up. He'd just eaten one of the best dinners he could ever remember and now he'd been turned upside-down and shaken without even being given time to explain.

Everyone exchanged glances and then crept quietly away, leaving Paddington to recover by himself. There didn't seem to be much they *could* say.

But after the dinner things had been cleared away, and by the time Mrs. Bird had made some strong coffee, Paddington was almost himself again. He was sitting up in the chair helping himself to some dates when they trooped back into the room. It took a lot to make Paddington ill for very long.

When they had finished their coffee, and were sitting round the blazing fire feeling warm and comfortable, Mr. Brown rubbed his hands. "Now, Paddington," he said, "it's not only Christmas, it's your birthday as well. What would you like to do?"

A mysterious expression came over Paddington's face.

"If you all go in the other room," he announced, "I've a special surprise for you."

"Oh dear, *must* we, Paddington?" said Mrs. Brown. "There isn't a fire."

"I shan't be long," said Paddington, firmly. "But it's a special surprise and it has to be prepared." He held the door open and the Browns, Mrs. Bird, and Mr. Gruber filed obediently into the other room.

"Now close your eyes," said Paddington, when they were settled, "and I'll let you know when I'm ready."

Mrs. Brown shivered. "I hope you won't be too long," she called. But the only reply was the sound of the door clicking shut.

They waited for several minutes without speaking, and then Mr. Gruber cleared his throat. "Do you think young Mr. Brown's forgotten about us?" he asked.

"I don't know," said Mrs. Brown. "But I'm not waiting much longer."

"Henry!" she exclaimed, as she opened her eyes. "Have you gone to sleep?"

"Er, wassat?" snorted Mr. Brown. He had eaten such a large dinner he was finding it difficult to keep awake. "What's happening? Have I missed anything?"

"Nothing's happening," said Mrs. Brown. "Henry, you'd better go and see what Paddington's up to."

Several more minutes went by before Mr. Brown returned to announce that he couldn't find Paddington anywhere.

"Well, he must be *somewhere*," said Mrs. Brown. "Bears don't disappear into thin air."

"Crikey!" exclaimed Jonathan, as a thought suddenly struck him. "You don't think he's playing at Father Christmas, do you? He was asking all about it the other day when he put his list up the chimney. I bet that's why he wanted us to come in here — because this chimney connects with the one upstairs, and there isn't a fire."

"Father Christmas?" said Mr. Brown. "I'll give him Father Christmas!" He stuck his head up the chimney and called Paddington's name several times. "I can't see anything," he said, striking a match. As if in answer a large lump of soot descended and burst on top of his head.

"Now look what you've done, Henry," said Mrs. Brown. "Shouting so — you've disturbed the soot. All over your clean shirt!"

"If it *is* young Mr. Brown, perhaps he's stuck somewhere," suggested Mr. Gruber. "He did have rather a large dinner. I remember wondering at the time where he put it all."

Mr. Gruber's suggestion had an immediate effect on the party and everyone began to look serious.

"Why, he might suffocate with the fumes," exclaimed Mrs. Bird, as she hurried outside to the broom cupboard.

When she returned, armed with a mop, everyone took it in turns to poke it up the chimney but even though they strained their ears they couldn't hear a sound.

It was while the excitement was at its height that Paddington came into the room. He looked most surprised when he saw Mr. Brown with his head up the chimney.

"You can come into the dining room now," he announced, looking round the room. "I've finished wrapping my presents and they're all on the Christmas tree."

"You don't mean to say," sputtered Mr. Brown, as he sat in the fireplace rubbing his face with a handkerchief, "you've been in the other room all the time?"

"Yes," said Paddington, innocently. "I hope I didn't keep you waiting too long."

Mrs. Brown looked at her husband. "I thought you said you'd looked everywhere," she exclaimed.

"Well — we'd just come from the dining room," said Mr. Brown, looking very sheepish. "I didn't think he'd be *there*."

"It only goes to show," said Mrs. Bird hastily, as she caught sight of the expression on Mr. Brown's face, "how easy it is to give a bear a bad name."

Paddington looked most interested when they explained to him what all the fuss was about.

"I never thought of coming down the chimney," he said, staring at the fireplace.

"Well, you're not thinking about it now either," replied Mr. Brown, sternly.

But even Mr. Brown's expression changed as he followed Paddington into the dining room and saw the presents that had been prepared for them.

In addition to the presents that had already been placed on the tree, there were now six newly wrapped ones tied to the lower branches. If the Browns recognized the wrapping paper they had used for Paddington's presents earlier in the day, they were much too polite to say anything.

"I'm afraid I had to use old paper," said Paddington apologetically, as he waved a paw at the tree. "I hadn't any money left. That's why you had to go in the other room while I wrapped them."

"Really, Paddington," said Mrs. Brown. "I'm very cross with you — spending all your money on presents for us."

"I'm afraid they're rather ordinary," said Paddington, as he settled back in a chair to watch the others. "But I hope you like them. They're all labeled so that you know which is which."

"Ordinary?" exclaimed Mr. Brown, as he opened his parcel. "I don't call a pipe rack ordinary. And there's an ounce of my favorite tobacco tied to the back as well!"

"Gosh! A new stamp album!" cried Jonathan. "Whizzo! And it's got some stamps inside already."

"They're Peruvian ones from Aunt Lucy's postcards," said Paddington. "I've been saving them for you."

"And I've got a box of paints," exclaimed Judy. "Thank you very much, Paddington. It's just what I wanted."

"We all seem to be lucky," said Mrs. Brown, as she unwrapped a parcel containing a bottle of her favorite lavender water. "How *did* you guess? I finished my last bottle only a week ago."

"I'm sorry about your parcel, Mrs. Bird," said Paddington, looking across the room. "I had a bit of a job with the knots."

"It must be something special," said Mr. Brown. "It seems all string and no parcel."

"That's because it's really clothes line," explained Paddington, "not string. I rescued it when I got stuck in the revolving door at Crumbold and Ferns."

"That makes two presents in one," said Mrs. Bird, as she freed the last of the knots and began unwinding yards and yards of paper. "How exciting. I can't think what it can be."

"Why," she exclaimed. "I do believe it's a brooch! And it's shaped like a bear — how lovely!" Mrs. Bird looked most touched as she handed the present round for everyone to see. "I shall keep it in a safe place," she added, "and only wear it on special occasions — when I want to impress people."

"I don't know what mine is," said Mr. Gruber, as they all turned to him. He squeezed the parcel. "It's such a funny shape."

"It's a drinking mug!" he exclaimed, his face lighting up with pleasure. "And it even has my name painted on the side!"

"It's for your morning cocoa, Mr. Gruber," said Paddington. "I noticed your old one was getting rather chipped."

"I'm sure it will make my cocoa taste better than it ever has before," said Mr. Gruber.

He stood up and cleared his throat. "I think I would like to offer a vote of thanks to young Mr. Brown," he said, "for all his nice presents. I'm sure he must have given them a great deal of thought."

"Hear! Hear!" echoed Mr. Brown, as he filled his pipe.

Mr. Gruber felt under his chair, "And while I think of it, Mr. Brown, I have a small present for you."

Everyone stood round and watched while Paddington struggled with his parcel, eager to see what Mr. Gruber had bought him. A gasp of surprise went up as he tore the paper to one side, for it was a beautifully bound leather scrapbook, with "Paddington Brown" printed in gold leaf on the cover.

Paddington didn't know what to say, but Mr. Gruber waved his thanks to one side. "I know how you enjoy writing about your adventures, Mr. Brown," he said, "and you have so many I'm sure your present scrapbook must be almost full."

"It is," said Paddington, earnestly. "And I'm sure I

shall have lots more. Things happen to me, you know. But I shall only put my best ones in here!"

When he made his way up to bed later that evening, his mind was in such a whirl, and he was so full of good things, he could hardly climb the stairs — let alone think about anything. He wasn't quite sure which he had enjoyed most. The presents, the Christmas dinner, the games, or the tea — with the special marmalade-layer birthday cake Mrs. Bird had made in his honor. Pausing on the corner half way up, he decided he had enjoyed giving his own presents best of all.

Michael Bond

cosette's christmas

Cosette, a little orphan girl, is a servant in the Thénardiers' tavern. They abuse her and make her life miserable.

O ne Christmas evening, several men, wagon-drivers and peddlers, were seated at table and drinking around four or five candles in the low hall of the Thénardier inn. This room resembled all taverns: tables, pewter mugs, bottles, drinkers, smokers, little light, and much noise. The date, 1823, was however, indicated by the two things then in style in middle-class families: on the table were a kaleidoscope and a fluted tin lamp. Thénardier, the wife, was looking to the supper, which was cooking before a bright, blazing fire; the husband, Thénardier, was drinking with his guests and talking politics.

Cosette was at her usual place, seated on the crosspiece of the kitchen table, near the fireplace. She was clad in

rags, her bare feet were in wooden shoes, and by the light of the fire she was knitting woolen stockings for the little Thénardiers.

Cosette was musing sadly; for though she was only eight years old, she had already suffered so much that she mused with the mournful air of an old woman.

Cosette was then thinking that it was evening, late in the evening, that the bowls and pitchers in the rooms of the travelers who had arrived must be filled immediately, and that there was no more water in the cistern. Mrs. Thénardier raised the cover of a kettle which was boiling on the range, then took a glass and hastily approached the cistern. She turned the faucet; the child had raised her head and followed all her movements. A thin stream of water ran from the faucet and filled the glass half full.

"Here," said she, "there is no more water!" Then she was silent for a moment. The child held her breath.

Mrs. Thénardier threw the street door wide open.

"Well, go after some!"

Cosette hung her head, and went for an empty bucket that was by the chimney corner.

The bucket was larger than she, and the child could have sat down in it comfortably.

Mrs. Thénardier went back to her range and tasted what was in the kettle with a wooden spoon, grumbling all the while.

"There is some at the spring. She is the worst girl that ever was. I think 'twould have been better if I'd left out the onions."

Then she fumbled in a drawer where there were some pennies, pepper, and garlic.

"Here, Mam'zelle Toad," added she, "get a big loaf at the baker's as you come back. Here is fifteen sous."

Cosette had a little pocket in the side of her apron; she took the piece without saying a word, and put it in that pocket.

Then she remained motionless, bucket in hand, the open door before her. She seemed to be waiting for somebody to come to her aid.

"Get along!" cried Mrs. Thénardier.

Cosette went out. The door closed.

★　★　★

There was a fair in the village with all sorts of booths.

The last of these stalls, set up exactly opposite Thénardier's door, was a toy shop, all glittering with trinkets, glass beads, and magnificent things in tin. In the first row, right in front, the merchant had placed, upon a bed of white napkins, a great doll nearly two feet high wearing a dress of pink crepe. It had golden birds on its head, and real hair and enamel eyes.

At the moment when Cosette went out, bucket in hand, all gloomy and overwhelmed as she was, she could not help raising her eyes toward this wonderful doll, toward *the lady*, as she called it. The poor child stopped petrified. She had not seen this doll so near before.

This whole booth seemed a palace to her; this doll was not a doll, it was a vision. She gazed upon this beautiful pink dress, this beautiful smooth hair, and she was thinking, "How happy that doll must be!"

In this adoration, she forgot everything, even the errand on which she had been sent. Suddenly, the harsh voice of Mrs. Thénardier called her back to reality: "How, jade, haven't you gone yet? Hold on; I am coming for you! I'd like to know what she's doing there! Little monster, be off!"

Mrs. Thénardier had glanced into the street, and perceived Cosette in ecstasy.

Cosette fled with her bucket, running as fast as she could.

As the Thénardier tavern was in that part of the village which is near the church, Cosette had to go to the spring in the woods toward Chelles to draw water.

The further she went, the thicker became the darkness. There was no longer anybody in the street. She ran out of the village; she ran into the woods, seeing nothing, hearing nothing. She did not stop running until she was out of breath, and even then she staggered on. She went right on, desperate.

Thus she arrived at the spring. Cosette did not take time to breathe. It was very dark, but she was accustomed to coming to this fountain. She bent down and plunged the bucket in the water. She was for a moment so excited that her strength tripled. When she was thus bent over, she did not notice that the pocket of her apron emptied itself into the spring. The fifteen sous piece fell into the water. Cosette neither saw it nor heard it fall. She drew out the bucket almost full and set it on the grass. She grasped the handle with both hands. She could hardly lift the bucket. After resting a few seconds, she started on.

Arriving near an old chestnut tree which she knew, she made a last halt, longer than the others, to get well rested; then she gathered all her strength, took up the bucket again, and began to walk on courageously. Meanwhile the poor little despairing thing could not help crying: "Oh my God! my God!"

At that moment she felt all at once that the weight of the bucket was gone. A hand, which seemed enormous to her, had just caught the handle, and was carrying it easily. She raised her head. A large dark form, straight and erect, was walking beside her in the gloom. It was a man who had come up behind her, and whom she had not heard. This man, without saying a word, had grasped the handle of the bucket she was carrying.

"What is your name?" said the man.

"Cosette."

"Who is it that has sent you out into the woods after water at this time of the night?"

"Madame Thénardier."

"What does she do, your Madame Thénardier?"

"She is my mistress," said the child. "She keeps the tavern."

"The tavern," said the man. "Well I am going there to lodge tonight. Show me the way."

As they drew near the tavern, Cosette timidly touched his arm:

"Monsieur?"

"What, my child?"

"Here we are, close by the house."

"Well?"

"Will you let me take the bucket now?"

"What for?"

"Because, if madame sees that anybody brought it for me, she will beat me."

The man gave her the bucket. A moment after they were at the door of the chophouse.

"Madame," said Cosette, trembling, "here is a gentleman who is coming to lodge."

"Ah! My brave man, I am very sorry, but I have no room."

"Put me where you will," said the man, "in the garret, in the stable. I will pay as if I had a room."

"Forty sous."

"Forty sous. Well."

"In advance."

"Forty sous," whispered a wagon-driver to Mrs. Thénardier, "but it is only twenty sous."

"It is forty sous for him," replied Mrs. Thénardier in the same tone. "I don't lodge poor people for less."

"That is true," added the husband softly, "it ruins a house to have this sort of people."

Meanwhile, the man, after leaving his stick and bundle on a bench, had seated himself at a table on which Cosette had been quick to place a bottle of wine and a glass.

Suddenly, Mrs. Thénardier exclaimed:

"Oh I forgot! The bread!"

Cosette, according to her custom whenever Mrs. Thénardier raised her voice, sprang out quickly from under the table.

She had entirely forgotten the bread. She acted as do children who are always terrified. She lied.

"Madame, the baker was closed."

"You ought to have knocked."

"I did knock, Madame."

"Well?"

"He didn't open."

"I'll find out tomorrow if that is true," said Mrs. Thénardier, "and if you are lying you will lead a pretty dance. Meantime, give me back the fifteen sous piece."

Cosette plunged her hand into her apron pocket, and turned white. The fifteen sous piece was not there.

"Come," said the woman, "didn't you hear me?"

Cosette turned her pocket inside out; there was nothing there. What could have become of that money? The little unfortunate could not utter a word. She was petrified.

"Have you lost it, the fifteen sous piece?" screamed the woman, "or do you want to steal it from me?"

At the same time she reached her arm toward the cow-hide whip hanging in the chimney corner.

This menacing movement gave Cosette the strength to cry out:

"Forgive me! Madame! Madame! I won't do so any more!"

The woman took down the whip.

Meanwhile the man in the yellow coat had been fumbling in his waistcoat pocket, without being noticed. The other travelers were drinking or playing cards, and paid no attention to anything.

Cosette was writhing with anguish in the chimney corner, trying to gather up and hide her poor half-naked limbs. Mrs. Thénardier raised her arm.

"I beg your pardon, Madame," said the man, "but I just now saw something fall out of the pocket of that little girl's apron and roll away. That may be it."

At the same time he stooped down and appeared to search on the floor for an instant.

"Just so, here it is," said he rising.

And he handed a silver piece to the woman.

"Yes, that is it," said she.

That was not it, for it was a twenty sous piece, but Mrs. Thénardier found her profit in it. She put the piece in her pocket, and contented herself with casting a ferocious look at the child and saying:

"Don't let that happen again, ever."

Cosette went back to what Mrs. Thénardier called "her hole," and her large eyes, fixed upon the unknown traveler, began to assume an expression that they had never known before. It was still only an artless astonishment, but a sort of blind confidence was associated with it.

A door now opened, and Eponine and Azelma came in.

They were really two pretty little girls, rather city girls than peasants, very charming, one with her well-polished auburn tresses, the other with her long black braids falling down on her back, and both so lively, neat, plump, fresh, and healthy, that it was a pleasure to see them.

They went and sat down by the fire. They had a doll which they turned backward and forward upon their knees with many pretty prattlings. From time to time, Cosette raised her eyes from her knitting, and looked sadly at them as they were playing.

Eponine and Azelma did not notice Cosette. To them she was like the dog. The doll of the Thénardier sisters was very much faded, and very old and broken; but it appeared none the less wonderful to Cosette who had never in her life had a doll, *a real doll.*

Cosette had left her knitting, but she had not moved

from her place. Cosette always stirred as little as possible. She had taken from a little box behind her a few old rags, and her little lead sword.

Eponine and Azelma paid no attention to what was going on. They had just performed a very important operation; they had caught the kitten. They had thrown the doll on the floor.

While Eponine and Azelma were dressing up the cat, Cosette, for her part, had dressed up the sword. That done, she had laid it upon her arm, and was singing it softly to sleep.

All at once, Cosette stopped. She had just turned and seen the little Thénardiers' doll, which they had forsaken for the cat and left on the floor, a few steps from the kitchen table.

Then she let the bundled-up sword, which only half satisfied her, fall, and ran her eyes slowly around the room. Mrs. Thénardier was whispering to her husband and counting some money; Eponine and Azelma were playing with the cat; the travelers were eating and drinking or singing; nobody was looking at her. She had not a moment to lose. She crept out from under the table on her hands and knees, made sure once more that nobody was watching her, then she darted quickly to the doll, and seized her. An instant afterwards she was at her place, seated, motionless, only turned in such a way as to keep the doll that she held in her arms in the shadow.

Nobody had seen her, except the traveler, who was slowly eating his meager supper.

This joy lasted for nearly a quarter of an hour.

But in spite of Cosette's precautions, she did not perceive that one of the doll's feet stuck out, and that the fire in the fireplace lighted it up vividly. This rosy and luminous foot which protruded from the shadow suddenly caught Azelma's eye, and she said to Eponine: "Oh, sister!"

The two little girls stopped, stupefied; Cosette had dared to take the doll.

Eponine got up and, without letting go of the cat, went to her mother and began to pull at her skirt.

"Let me alone," said the mother; "what do you want?"

"Mother," said the child, "look there."

And she pointed at Cosette.

Cosette, wholly absorbed in the ecstasy of her possession, saw and heard nothing else.

"Cosette!"

Cosette shuddered as if the earth had quaked beneath her. She turned around.

"Cosette!" repeated Mrs. Thénardier.

Cosette took the doll and placed it gently on the floor, with a kind of veneration mingled with despair. She sobbed.

Meanwhile the traveler rose. "What is the matter?" he asked.

"Don't you see?" answered the woman.

"Well, what is that?" said the man.

"That beggar has dared to touch the children's doll."

"Well, what if she did play with that doll?"

"She has touched it with her dirty hands!" continued Mrs. Thénardier, "with her horrid hands!"

Here Cosette redoubled her sobs.

"Be still!" cried the woman.

The man walked straight to the street door, opened it, and went out.

As soon as he was gone Mrs. Thénardier profited by his absence to give Cosette under the table a severe kick, which made the child shriek.

The door opened again, and the man reappeared, holding in his hands the fabulous doll of which we have spoken, and which had been the admiration of all the youngsters of the village since morning; he stood it up before Cosette, saying:

"Here, this is for you."

Cosette raised her eyes; she saw the man approach her with the doll as she would have seen the sun approach, she heard those astounding words: *This is for you.* She looked at him, she looked at the doll, then she drew back slowly, and went and hid as far as she could under the table in the corner of the room.

She wept no more, she cried no more, she had the appearance of no longer daring to breathe.

Mrs. Thénardier, Eponine, and Azelma were so many statues. Even the drinkers stopped. There was a solemn silence in the whole room.

Cosette looked upon the wonderful doll with a sort of terror. It seemed to her that if she touched that doll, thunder would spring forth from it. Which was true to some extent, for she thought that Mrs. Thénardier would scold and beat her.

However the attraction overcame her. She finally approached and timidly murmured, turning toward Mrs. Thénardier:

"Can I, Madame?"

"Good Lord!" said the woman. "It is yours, since Monsieur gives it to you."

"Is it true, is it true, Monsieur?" Cosette asked. "Is the lady for me?"

The stranger appeared to have his eyes full of tears. He nodded assent to Cosette, and put the hand of "the lady" in her little hand.

"I will call her Catharine," said she.

It was Eponine and Azelma now who looked upon Cosette with envy.

Cosette went to bed, holding Catharine in her arms.

Several hours passed away. The midnight mass was said, the revel was finished, the drinkers had gone, the house was closed, the room was deserted, the fire had gone out, the stranger still remained in the same place and in the same posture.

The innkeeper retired to his room; his wife was in bed but not asleep. When she heard her husband's step, she turned toward him, and said:

"You know that I am going to kick Cosette outdoors tomorrow!"

For his part, the traveler had put his staff and bundle in a corner. The host gone, he sat down in an armchair, and there he remained for some time, thinking. Then he drew off his shoes, and went out of the room, looking about him as if he were searching for something. He passed through the hall, and came to the stairway. There he heard a very soft little sound, which resembled the breathing of a child. There, among all sorts of old baskets and old rubbish, in the dust and among the cobwebs, there was a bed — if a mattress so full of holes as to show the straw, and a covering so full of holes as to show the mattress, can be called a bed. There were no sheets. This was placed on the floor immediately on the tiles. In this bed Cosette was sleeping.

The man approached and looked at her.

Cosette was sleeping soundly; she was dressed. In the winter she did not undress on account of the cold. She held the doll clasped in her arms.

On the following morning, at least two hours before day, Thénardier, seated at a table in the barroom, a candle by his side, with pen in hand, was making out the bill of the traveler in the yellow coat. His wife was standing, half bent over him, following with her eyes.

"You don't forget that I kick Cosette out of the house today? The monster! It tears me apart to see her with her doll!"

Thénardier lighted his pipe and answered between two puffs:

"You'll give the bill to the man."

Then he went out.

He was scarcely out of the room when the traveler came in.

Mrs. Thénardier handed him the folded bill.

The man unfolded the paper and looked at it; but his thoughts were evidently elsewhere.

"Madame," replied he, "do you do a good business in Montfermeil?"

"So-so, Monsieur," answered Mrs. Thénardier, stupefied at seeing no other explosion.

She continued in a mournful and lamenting train:

"Oh! Monsieur, the times are very hard, and then we have so few rich people around here! It is a very little place, you see. If we only had rich travelers now and then, like Monsieur! We have so many expenses! Why, that little girl eats us out of house and home."

"What little girl?"

"Why, the little girl you know! Cosette!"

"Suppose you were relieved of her?"

"Who? Cosette?"

"Yes."

"Ah, Monsieur! my good monsieur! Take her, keep her, take her away, carry her off, sugar her, stuff her, drink her, eat her, and be blessed by the holy Virgin and all the saints in Paradise!"

"Agreed."

"Really! you will take her away?"

"I will."

"Immediately?"

"Immediately. Call the child."

"Cosette!" cried the woman.

"In the meantime," continued the man, "I will pay my bill. How much is it?"

He cast a glance at the bill, and could not repress a movement of surprise.

"Twenty-three francs?"

He looked at the hostess and repeated, "Twenty-three francs?"

Mrs. Thénardier had had time to prepare herself for the shock. She replied with assurance;

"Yes, of course, Monsieur! It is twenty-three francs."

The stranger placed five five-franc pieces upon the table.

"Go for the little girl," said he.

At this moment Thénardier advanced in the middle of the room and said:

"Monsieur owes twenty-six sous."

"Twenty-six sous!" exclaimed the woman.

"Twenty sous for the room," continued Thénardier coldly, "and six for supper. As to the little girl, I must have some talk with Monsieur about that. Leave us, Wife."

Thénardier continued, "How strangely we become attached! What is all this silver? Take back your money. This child I adore."

"Who is that?" asked the stranger.

"Oh, our little Cosette. Pardon me, excuse me, Monsieur, but one does not give his child like that to a traveler. 1 do not know even your name. I must, at least see some poor rag of paper, a bit of a passport, something."

The stranger, without removing from him this gaze which went, so to speak, to the bottom of his conscience, answered in a severe and firm tone:

"Monsieur Thénardier, people do not take a passport to come five leagues from Paris. If I take Cosette, I take her, that is all. You will not know my name, you will not know my abode, you will not know where she goes, and my intention is that she shall never see you again in her life. Do you agree to that? Yes or no?"

"Monsieur," said he, "I must have fifteen hundred francs."

The stranger took from his side pocket an old black leather pocketbook, opened it, and drew forth three bank bills which he placed upon the table. He then rested his large thumb on these bills, and said to the tavern keeper:

"Bring Cosette."

The day was breaking when those of the inhabitants of Montfermeil who were beginning to open their doors, saw pass on the road to Paris a poorly clad good man leading a little girl, dressed in mourning, who had a pink doll in her arms.

It was the stranger and Cosette.

Cosette walked seriously along, opening her large eyes, and looking at the sky. From time to time she looked at the good man. She felt somewhat as if she were near God.

Victor Hugo

The Christmas Spider

The gray spider worked very hard every day making long strands of silk that he wove into a web in which he caught troublesome flies. But he noticed that everyone turned away from him because, they said, he was so unpleasant to look at with his long, crooked legs and furry body. Of course the gray spider didn't believe that, because he had only the kindliest feelings for everybody. One day when he was crossing the stream he looked into the water. There he saw himself as he really was.

"Oh," he thought, "I *am* very unpleasant to look at. I shall keep out of people's way." He was very sad and hid himself in the darkest corner of the stable. There he again began to work as he always had, weaving long strands of silk into webs and catching flies. The donkey and the ox and the sheep who lived in the stable thanked him for his kindness, because now they were no longer bothered with the buzzing flies. That made the spider very happy.

One night, exactly at midnight, the spider was awakened by a brilliant light. He looked about and saw that the light came from the manger where a tiny Child lay on the hay. The stable was filled with glory, and over the Child bent a beautiful mother. Behind her stood a man with a staff in his hand, and the ox and the donkey and all the white sheep were down on their knees.

Suddenly a gust of cold wind swept through the stable and the Baby began to weep from the cold. The mother bent over Him but could not cover Him enough to keep Him warm. The little spider took his silken web and laid it at Mary's feet (for it was Mary), and Mary took up the web and covered the Baby with it. It was soft as thistledown and as warm as wool. The Child stopped his crying and smiled at the little gray spider.

Then Mary said, "Little gray spider, for this great gift to the Babe you may have anything you wish."

"Most of all," said the spider, "I wish to be beautiful."

"That I cannot give you," Mary answered. "You must stay as you are for as long as you live. But this I grant you. Whenever anyone sees a spider at evening, he will count it a good omen, and it shall bring him good fortune."

This made the spider very happy, and to this day, on Christmas Eve, we cover the Christmas tree with "angel's hair" in memory of the gray spider and his silken web.

Marguerite de Angeli

The Christmas Gift

It was Christmas Eve—and, except for Mr. Wilson, every member of the Wilson family was sharing in the fun of trimming the big fragrant fir tree that stood in the bay window. Even the baby in his playpen was enjoying the excitement of tinsel and tree lights, icicles and ornaments, and packages, packages, everywhere!

But Mr. Wilson, alone in the hallway, clutched the telephone in his hand, scarcely believing the words that came crackling over the line.

"Usually," the polite voice was saying, "in an emergency of this sort we arrange space with the airport motel for off-loaded passengers. But we knew the little girl was going to a hospital in Minneapolis, and we thought she might need special care a motel couldn't give. Then when she told us she spent last night at your home, we knew our problem was solved. Of course we'll have her driven to your address."

Mr. Wilson managed to say politely, "You did exactly the right thing. Thank you, and good-bye." Then he put down the phone and sighed heavily.

"Of all places for Ella Mae Growthers to spend Christmas Eve, it has to be here," he muttered. "That kid!"

He could see Ella Mae again, straw-colored hair straggling, dark eyes snapping, hunched over her crutches at the airlines terminal magazine stand. He'd asked her what magazine she would like to look at on the plane.

"Look at a *magazine!*" Ella Mae had replied, loudly and scornfully. "Git me a seat so's I can look out a *window.* I'm taking a trip, ain't I?"

"Everything anybody tries to do for Ella Mae is a flop," Mr. Wilson thought. "Some merry addition that kid will be to our Christmas. Well, I might as well get the bad news over with."

In the living-room doorway he paused, his eyes suddenly focused on Jenny, the "middle" Wilson. Kneeling by the tree, she was carefully draping icicles along the boughs. Jenny — exactly Ella Mae's age! A sudden flush came over Mr. Wilson's face. What if it was Jenny at the airport — a Jenny nobody wanted? Just then, she turned her head. "Come on in, Daddy. You haven't helped a bit yet!"

"How about keeping this steady for me, Dad?" Tod called from the top of the ladder. "My Helping Hand isn't much help." He grinned down at Carol, his twin sister.

"Much help! Who's not much help? When I said give the baby a spool to play with, I meant an *empty* spool," Carol answered. "Look at your youngest son, Dad."

Johnny, wreathed and tangled in red satin ribbon, staggered along the bars of his playpen, squealing excitedly.

Mrs. Wilson looked up at her husband. "Who was that calling, dear?"

"The airport," Mr. Wilson replied. "Tod, you're going

to have to clip that top or the star will scratch the ceiling."

"Why on earth was the airport calling?" Mrs. Wilson asked. Suddenly she put down the package she was wrapping. "Don't tell me something's gone wrong with Ella Mae's flight!"

"Ella Mae's flight never got off the ground," Mr. Wilson said gloomily. "After we put her on the plane and left, word came through that Minneapolis is socked in. No planes can land. Big blizzard. Anyhow, the airlines people learned from Ella Mae that she'd been staying with us. So now they will have somebody drive the child back here."

"I'll bet they will!" Carol exclaimed. "They probably can't wait to get that kid off their hands."

Tod clipped the star into place and started down the ladder. "Dad, you aren't the only member of the Crippled Children's Committee in town," he said. "How come *this* family is always the one to get the overnight visitors? And two nights of Ella Mae — wow!"

Even Mrs. Wilson looked cross. "Well, it *is* too bad, Richard," she said. "Christmas is a time for families to be close together. Carol and Tod home from college for just a few days, and Jenny wanting her room to herself, and all of us wrapping Christmas presents. *Presents!* What on earth will we do about presents for Ella Mae? After all, we can't all be gaily unwrapping gifts Christmas morning with that child just *looking on*. We can't leave her out of things no matter if she is, well — difficult."

"It looks to me as though Ella Mae has already been left

out of things," Mr. Wilson said quietly. "There was a reason the Committee scheduled this trip for the 24th. The district nurse told me that at least Ella Mae might get in on the fun of the Hospital's annual Christmas party. She'd have *that* much, anyhow, in between now and her operation."

Then Jenny, who hadn't said one word up to now, suddenly burst into action. She jumped up, her face nearly as red as the ruby Christmas ornaments she held, and turned to her father. "You can be sorry for her if you want to, Daddy. But *you* don't have to share your room with a messy kid, and have all your things wrecked. And *you* aren't just her age, like me. I don't care if she *is* on crutches and wears braces. She's mean. She's the meanest kid I ever saw. *And I hate her!*" With that, Jenny hurled the tree ornaments straight across the room. They bounced, rolled airily, then smashed into sharp, curving fragments against chair, tables, and the piano.

"Jenny!" everybody exclaimed at once. And Jenny burst into tears and ran at top speed out of the room. Immediately, the baby began to wail.

Mrs. Wilson lifted up the sobbing youngest member of the family, and jiggled him soothingly. "Carol, dear, would you get the dustpan? And better bring some wet paper toweling too. We want to be sure no sharp pieces are left on the rug."

"Why can't Jenny do it?" Carol asked grumpily.

"Jenny seems to have all the problems she can stand," Mrs. Wilson replied. "I'm ashamed to say it, but I almost feel like throwing things myself. Ella Mae is no Tiny Tim from *A Christmas Carol,* I must say."

Tod burst out laughing. "I can just hear Ella Mae saying, 'God bless us, each and every one.' " He shook his head. "That's a kid only her mother could love."

"Maybe that's part of the trouble," Mr. Wilson said. "She doesn't have one."

Mrs. Wilson stared, then gently brushed her cheek against the baby's silky hair. She looked at her husband. "Richard," she said softly, "I guess where you're concerned there's always 'room at the inn' isn't there? And I'm proud of you for it."

Mr. Wilson turned red. "Well don't think I was filled with joy or anything. She's a hard kid to have around. I admit it. But —" He broke off. "Say, she'll be here any minute. What do we do about presents?"

Mrs. Wilson sighed. "One thing at a time, dear. Let me get the baby to bed first. And I'm sending Jenny back downstairs." She looked at Carol and Tod. "Jenny doesn't deserve any congratulations for that performance — but just remember, she only did what most of us *felt* like doing."

By the time the doorbell rang and the airline's hostess handed Ella Mae over to the Wilsons, the rug had been brushed clean, packages had been stacked under the fragrant boughs of the tree, the baby was sound asleep upstairs, and Jenny was in the kitchen silently stuffing walnuts into dates and rolling them in powdered sugar.

"Merry Christmas, Ella Mae!" Mrs. Wilson said cheerfully. "Here, let me help you off with your coat."

Ella Mae's coal-dark eyes flashed. "Take my crutches," she said angrily. "And one at a time. I'll take off my own coat."

"Wait until you see our tree, Ella Mae," Carol said hastily. "It's just beautiful."

"Wait? That's what I been doing ever since I struck this town — wait. Right now I'm *supposed* to be riding on a airplane to Minneapolis." She shrugged her arm out of the coat sleeve. "Gimme back my crutches. Where's the tree?"

Carol led the way into the living room and Tod, with Mr. and Mrs. Wilson, trailed behind Ella Mae. Her crutches sprangled out on either side, hitting table legs and sending lamps into wild wobbles. She swung herself toward the tree — and stared. It *was* a beautiful tree, glowing and twinkling and smelling so nice.

"What do you think of it, Ella Mae?" Mr. Wilson asked.

Ella Mae swallowed. "They got one as good at the airport. I seen it." She swung around again. "Where's your other kid?" she asked. "Jenny."

"Hard at work in the kitchen making stuffed dates," Mrs. Wilson replied. "I'll call her — or would you like to go out and help?"

"You needn't bother either whichway," Ella Mae answered in a hard voice. "I'd druther get to bed."

There was a quick silence, then Tod said, "It's Christmas Eve and usually we sing some carols, get out the guitars — stuff like that. How about it? We wish you'd stick around."

A sudden glint had come into Ella Mae's eyes. "Did you say *gee-tars*? You mean you got more'n one?"

Tod nodded. "I have one and Carol has one."

"Are they plug-ins?" Ella Mae asked. "I never seen me a plug-in but on the TV."

Tod and Carol exchanged glances. "Oh — the electric kind," Carol said quickly. "No, but we have a lot of fun with them, anyhow."

"Jenny got one?" Ella Mae asked, looking sharply from Carol to Tod.

Tod grinned. "No. Jenny won't even sing. Says she can't. We think she's just fooling about that, though, because Mother says she sings up a storm around here when Carol and I are away at school."

Ella Mae glanced down at her heavy shoes, then looked up very quickly. "Maybe Jenny *can* sing nice," she said slowly. "It's hard when everybody is better'n you are."

The Wilsons looked swiftly at each other, then looked swiftly away. Carol cleared her throat. "I never thought of that. Did you, Tod?"

"Sure. Didn't you ever notice I never went out for basketball after the ninth grade? All the guys got to be about eight feet tall, and there I was — couldn't get past five-eleven stretching. For a while there, I wouldn't even go to a game."

Ella Mae hunched up on her crutches. "You mean you

go to them games now?" she asked, staring hard.

"Sure."

"How come you'd do that?"

Tod shrugged. "Gave up, I guess. Wasn't anything left to do but *enjoy* myself."

Mrs. Wilson spoke up. "Do you know it's already nine o'clock. I have a good idea. It's so comfortable sitting around in a robe just knowing that when you're sleepy all you'll have to do is tumble into bed. Tod, maybe you're not tall enough, but you're strong enough. How about taking Ella Mae upstairs — and back, of course. Then we'll sing carols."

As Mrs. Wilson went upstairs with Tod carrying Ella Mae and Carol following with the crutches and suitcase, Jenny came into the living room. She walked over to her father.

"Daddy, I'm sorry I smashed the tree ornaments," she said in a low voice.

Mr. Wilson turned toward the tree. "Carol cleaned everything up," he said quietly, and bent down to look at the gaily wrapped packages. "We still don't have any idea of what we can give Ella Mae."

Jenny hesitated. Then she held out a gift tag. "I wrote it out in the kitchen," she said. She swallowed hard. "I thought maybe you and Mother could — could — put it on the *right* present," she finished.

Mr. Wilson took the tag and read it aloud. " 'To our

friend Ella Mae, from all of the Wilson family.' Why, that's very nice, Jenny. I guess you know that Tod's and Carol's presents probably wouldn't be anywhere near right for Ella Mae, don't you?"

Jenny nodded. "I guess I can stand it," she sighed. "I guess maybe I can even stand Ella Mae. Maybe Christmas will soften her up or something."

"Or soften *us* up or something," her father smiled. "OK, honey. Thanks for the card. Why don't you go up and put on your robe and pajamas — sort of keep Ella Mae company?"

Jenny grinned. "What robe? I'll bet Ella Mae's wrapped up in mine right this minute."

"Oh, you'll think of something," her father grinned back. "And Jenny — thanks again. For the card, I mean."

With Tod and Carol playing their guitars, they sang all the carols and Ella Mae knew most of them. Then there was hot chocolate and there were twinkly frosted Christmas cookies in pine tree shapes and star shapes, and Jenny contributed a plate of her stuffed dates. And now it was nearly midnight.

Ella Mae put down her cup. "I made me up a song," she said shyly. "Not no Christmas carol, of course. It's more of just a winter song."

"Sing it for us," Tod said.

Ella Mae hesitated. She glanced at Jenny. "Everybody can do something," she said in an apologetic kind of voice. "Me — I play the gee-tar."

"Well, for goodness sake! Why didn't you say so," Carol exclaimed. "Here — take mine." She put it in Ella Mae's lap. "Come on. Let's hear it."

Ella Mae's dark eyes flashed. "Git ready," she said. She leaned forward and strummed a few expert chords. "This here gee-tar looks different than my Uncle Rafe's. But I see it works about as good." She looked up. "This here song is about what I seen once. It was right in town and we was late starting home up the mountain. There was lights at every corner and there was a lot of snow. But the rest" — Ella Mae glanced toward her crutches — "well that's made up. It's real short."

"What do you call it, 'Winter Song'?" Tod asked. " 'Winter Song' by Miss Ella Mae Growther, folks. Coming right up."

Ella Mae's chin lifted. "I call it 'Angel in the Snow,' " she said with dignity.

In the shadowed living room, the Christmas tree glowed soft, making blurry circles of light on boughs and gifts and the faces around the tree. Ella Mae's pale straw-straight hair fell forward as she bent over Carol's guitar. And in the soft light from the tree she was a lovely, glowing child. Her fingers struck a chord, and she looked up at them all. Then her voice rose, clear and sweet.

"I got a story
Of winter time, you know.
It's about the night I seen
The street light on the snow.

Like a diamond blanket
Snow lay in front of me, and
Diamonds, diamond, diamonds
Was all that I could see.

I run right through them glitters,
And I lay me down so fair,
And I sang me a song
'Twas a street light prayer.

O street light on the corner
Shine on me below
Where I'm making, careful,
An angel in the snow."

Ella Mae's fingers stopped. "That's my one song," she said
sternly. "So you needn't ask for no more."

Jenny jumped up. "It was just beautiful! I could just
see the diamonds — and I could see the angel in the snow."

The clock in the hallway began to chime. "Merry Christmas! Merry Christmas everybody." Mrs. Wilson cried.
"Darling, it *was* beautiful, just as Jenny said. Merry,
merry Christmas!"

In the deserted living room, Mr. Wilson sorted out Jenny's "special" Christmas present from beneath the tree
— a guitar for her very own.

Carefully, he replaced the tag marked, "Jenny — Merry
Christmas from Mother and Daddy," with the tag for Ella
Mae. He looked at Jenny's writing thoughtfully. *From the*

Wilson family. "But it's Jenny who is giving up her gift," he thought.

He strode over to the desk, found a Christmas card, and wrote:

> Dear Jenny,
>
> If you like Ella Mae's present, give me one quick wink — and I'll see that you have one just like it.
>
> > Special love this special Christmas Day,
> > Daddy

Restacking the package marked for Ella Mae, he propped the envelope marked "Jenny," on top, then walked to the hall doorway and turned off the lights. He hesitated a moment in the darkened room and his hand went back to the wall switch. Once again, the tree sprang into glowing, radiant life. And it seemed to him that, like this tree, the Christmas spirit had shone more brightly in the Wilson home tonight because of a tough little girl named Ella Mae.

Vic Crume

Angel in the Snow

Vic Crume

Linda S. Williams

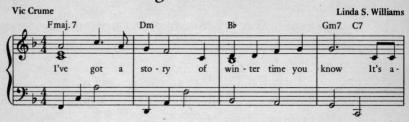

I've got a sto-ry of win-ter time you know It's a-

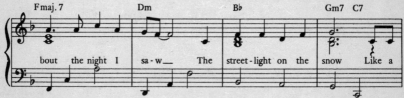

bout the night I sa-w_ The street-light on the snow Like a

dia - mond blan - ket snow lay in front of_ me And

dia-monds, dia-monds, di-a-monds were all that I could see I

ran right through those glit - ters And I lay_ me down so fair And I

110

F maj. 7   Dm   Gm   C7

sa - ng___ me a   song___   It was a street - light pray'r   Oh,

Bb   Gm7   Gm7   C7

street - light on the   cor - ner   shine on me be - low   Where

F   Dm   Gm7   C7

I am mak - ing care - ful - ly An   an - gel___ in the snow   Oh,

Gm7   C7   Gm7   C7   C+   F maj. 7

street - light on the   cor - ner   shine on me be - low   Where

Gm7   C7   Am   Dm   Gm7   C7   F

I am mak - ing care - ful - ly An   an - gel in the snow.___

I COULD EAT IT

I could eat it!
This snow that falls
       So softly,

        Kobayashi Issa